HOSTILE TERRAIN

Jim Eldridge was born in 1944 in London. He now lives in rural Cumbria with his wife. He has been writing for many years, most of his work being for television and radio. He is an award-winning writer, with over four hundred television and radio scripts broadcast and forty-five books published. His main interests outside writing are organic-vegetable gardening, reading, history and films.

HOSTILE TERRAIN

J. ELDRIDGE

A fictional story
based on real-life events

PUFFIN BOOKS

*To my wife, Lynne, for putting up
with the stress of my research*

PUFFIN BOOKS

Published by the Penguin Group
Penguin Books Ltd, 80 Strand, London WC2R 0RL, England
Penguin Putnam Inc., 375 Hudson Street, New York, New York 10014, USA
Penguin Books Australia Ltd, 250 Camberwell Road, Camberwell,
Victoria 3124, Australia
Penguin Books Canada Ltd, 10 Alcorn Avenue, Toronto, Ontario,
Canada M4V 3B2
Penguin Books India (P) Ltd, 11 Community Centre, Panchsheel Park,
New Delhi – 110 017, India
Penguin Books (NZ) Ltd, Cnr Rosedale and Airborne Roads,
Albany, Auckland, New Zealand
Penguin Books (South Africa) (Pty) Ltd, 24 Sturdee Avenue, Rosebank 2196,
South Africa

Penguin Books Ltd, Registered Offices: 80 Strand, London WC2R 0RL, England

www.penguin.com

First published 2003
1

Copyright © Jim Eldridge, 2003
All rights reserved

Although based on real-life events, all characters in this book are fictional.

The moral right of the author has been asserted

Set in Bookman Old Style

Made and printed in England by Clays Ltd, St Ives plc

British Library Cataloguing in Publication Data
A CIP catalogue record for this book is available from the British Library

ISBN 0–141–31589–X

CONTENTS

HISTORY OF THE
SAS

THE HISTORY OF THE SAS

The SAS developed from the Commandos of the British Army during the Second World War. David Stirling was a lieutenant in the Commandos fighting in the deserts of North Africa in 1941. He believed that a small group of men working covertly behind enemy lines could have a devastating effect. His idea was given official approval and so the Special Air Service was born. The newly formed SAS, just sixty-five men strong, carried out its first operation in November 1941, hitting enemy-held airfields on the North African coast. It worked with such effectiveness against the German forces in the deserts of North Africa that, in September 1942, the SAS was raised to full regiment status, 1 SAS Regiment – with a force of 650 men divided into four combat squadrons: A, B, C (the Free French Squadron) and D (the SBS, or Special Boat Section).

In 1943 an additional regiment, 2 SAS, was

created. Both regiments fought in the Allied invasion of Italy and Sicily in 1943, and then took part in the D-Day landings of June 1944, fighting behind enemy lines.

After the end of the Second World War, the SAS was disbanded. However, many ex-SAS men, who had seen the advantages of such a force, lobbied the War Office for its reinstatement in the British Army. The result was that, in 1947, an SAS unit, the Artists Rifles, was formed as part of the Territorial Army. Its official title was 21 SAS (Artists) TA, and many ex-SAS soldiers joined this new outfit. However, the military top brass reduced the SAS in size and importance. Many of the top brass did not like what they considered to be an 'unorthodox organization' within the ranks. By 1949 the SAS consisted of just two squadrons and a signals detachment.

Then, in 1950, came the Malayan conflict. Malaya had been under British control for many years. In 1948 Britain had set up the Federation of Malaya as a step towards independence. However, the minority Chinese population of Malaya, backed by Communist China, resented the domination of the federation by Malay people. Calling themselves the MRLA (Malayan Races Liberation Army),

2

they began a campaign against the British and Malays. During 1950 the MRLA killed 344 civilians and 229 soldiers.

Mike Calvert had fought with Orde Wingate's Chindits behind enemy lines in the Burmese jungle in the Second World War. He had ended the war as Commander of the SAS and he was given the task of reforming it into a fighting unit to deal with the MRLA. In 1950 Calvert set up a force known as the Malaya Scouts (SAS). This was made up of men from B Company, 21 SAS; C Squadron from Rhodesia (now called Zimbabwe), and some reservists. In 1952 the Malaya Scouts became officially known as 22 SAS. 22 SAS fought so successfully behind enemy lines in the jungles of Malaya – living and working with the local peoples – that by 1956 the leaders of the MRLA had fled to Thailand. The Malaya campaign came to an end in 1960, with the SAS having proved itself and its techniques of covert operations.

The strategic structure of an SAS Squadron had now been defined. An SAS Squadron consists of sixty-four men in sixteen four-man troops. Each troop has to be able to operate independently, living off the land. As well as being proficient in every kind of weapon and unarmed combat, the troop is capable of dealing with every possible medical emergency.

Further campaigns followed in which the SAS played a key role. In Aden and Borneo (1959–67) and in Oman (1970), SAS soldiers fought behind enemy lines – gaining the support of the local people and militia, blending into the scenery and attacking the enemy where least expected. During the 1970s and 1980s the SAS were major players in the war against terrorism in Northern Ireland. In 1982 the SAS played an important part in the Falklands War, and in 1991 in the Gulf War against Iraq.

Wherever war or terrorism threatens, the SAS is there.

SAS TRAINING – COLD CLIMATES

SAS cold climate training mainly takes place in the Arctic region of Norway. SAS soldiers train here every year. Additional cold climate training takes place at the German Mountain Warfare School in Mittenwald. The course at Mittenwald is divided into two parts: during the summer, mountain-climbing skills are refined and improved; and during the winter, skiing skills are developed. SAS Arctic warfare training exercises are also carried out in Canada.

As well as basic skiing, soldiers learn to carry their heavy bergen (rucksack) while on skis, and also to pull a pulk (a sled used for hauling equipment across snowy terrain). Soldiers also learn to use snow vehicles, such as the large Bandwagon and the two-man snowmobile.

The most important skill is learning to survive in extremes of cold weather. In cold climates, even when the sun is shining, temperatures can fall very quickly to as low as −40°C. Human skin freezes at −37°C. There is also the wind-chill factor to consider if the soldiers are to avoid suffering from frost-bite. For example, a 20mph wind can bring a temperature of −14°C down to a real temperature of −34°C. When being towed behind a vehicle the wind-chill factor can be even more hazardous: travelling at 20mph, when the air temperature is −20°C, produces a wind-chill on exposed skin of −43°C.

CLOTHING
Outer garments should be windproof but not waterproof, otherwise vapour gets trapped inside the clothing. Insulation is best provided by layers of undergarments, because warm air is trapped between the layers. The best material for undergarments is wool. It does not absorb moisture and even when it gets damp it stays warm, unlike cotton, which absorbs water and loses heat quite quickly.

SNOW-SHOES
Although skis are best on firm snow, snow-shoes are best on soft snow. To walk in snow-shoes, each shoe has to be kept as flat to the ground as possible (i.e., each foot has to be lifted without angling it).

NAVIGATION
Compasses are unreliable near the North and South Poles. It is dangerous to use ice-floes or icebergs to fix directions because they are constantly moving and

will give a false reading. For night travel, the star constellations in the sky are the best guide. For day travel, direction can be determined using the shadow stick method, as follows: Place a metre stick upright on a patch of flat ground. Mark where the tip of the shadow falls. After 15 minutes make a new mark showing where the tip of the shadow has moved to. Joining the two points will give you an east/west direction - the first mark you made being west, the second is east. North and south are at right angles to this line.

SHELTER

If you do not have a ready-made shelter (e.g., a tent), it is best to look for a natural shelter to build on. A snow trench (literally, a hole dug in snow big enough for one man to lie down in) will give protection against freezing winds.

A QUICK IGLOO

Normally, an igloo takes time to build, as well as skill in cutting and placing the blocks of snow and ice to construct it. A quick igloo can be made by stamping down an area of snow, then building a mound of hard, packed snow on top of it. When the mound is finished, tunnel into it.

Another quick method (only really suited to the Arctic where fire trees grow) is to build a frame of branches and pack snow on top of the frame.

Always make sure that the entrance to

your igloo is on the lee side (away from the direction of the wind). Ventilation is important, especially if you are using fire inside the shelter.

WATER

In Summer, melt ice and snow to get water. Do not put freezing ice straight into your mouth as this can cause injuries. It needs to be thawed first. Also, if you are already cold, eating snow and ice will add to the chill in your body.

HEALTH HAZARDS IN COLD CLIMATES

The three main health hazards in cold climates are hypothermia, frostbite, and snow-blindness.

HYPOTHERMIA

This occurs when the body brings the blood into its centre, and away from the extremities (head, feet, hands) to protect the vital organs.

SYMPTOMS

- Paleness
- Severe shivering
- Cold to the touch
- Fatigue
- Muscular weakness
- Drowsiness
- Disorientation
- Shallow breathing
- Faint heartbeat

TREATMENT

The aim is to stop further loss of heat from the body, and slowly replace the warmth already lost. This is done by insulating the body by wrapping in a blanket, adding as many layers as possible.

Anyone suffering from hypothermia should not be lifted suddenly vertically (e.g., dangling in a harness from a helicopter), because this will cause the blood immediately to leave the centre of the body and go to the feet. This will cause loss of blood from the vital organs at the centre of the body, resulting in death.

FROSTBITE

This can occur before the affected person is aware of it.

SYMPTOMS

- Pins and needles
- Tingling
- Stiffness
- Numbness
- Skin becomes grey or white in colour

TREATMENT

This is vital, because untreated frostbite leads to gangrene developing in the part of the body affected. This results in the affected part dying and having to be removed (e.g., hands, feet, etc have to be amputated). Treatment is similar to that for hypothermia: insulation against further body-heat loss and the slow warming of the skin. However, this only works in the early stages of frostbite, before the skin dies and gangrene sets in.

SNOW-BLINDNESS

This is caused by the glare of sun on snow. The effect is similar to having stared directly into the sun for a long period. To prevent snow blindness, protect the eyes with tinted goggles. If goggles are not available, use a strip of cloth wrapped around the head, covering the eyes, with narrow slits to see through. Also, the eyes can be blackened beneath (e.g. with soot from a fire) to reduce glare from the sun.

Chapter 1
INVASION

I froze as a branch snapped somewhere in the dense jungle on my left. It made the tiniest of sounds but it was enough to alert me that the terrorists were near by. I dropped to the ground immediately, signalling to Jake and Mack to do the same. Jerry, the fourth member of our squad, had been wounded. He was being carried, over the shoulder, fireman-style, by Mack, who rolled him on to the ground as he dropped down. I saw Jerry wince with pain, but not a sound passed his lips. Our lives depended on not being detected. The terrorist guerrillas tracking us had one mission – to find us and kill us.

I'm Rob Marshall. Ex-Marine, now a member of D Squadron, SAS. Being a member of the SAS meant I was used to extreme situations, and being in danger was just part of the job. But as I crouched silently on the jungle floor, hardly daring to breath, I wondered if it could get any worse. I tensed as I heard more movement on my right and faint whispers not far away. My guess was that there were at least five or six terrorists creeping towards us. Had they spotted us? Should we take them out now, before they got too near? My mind raced trying to figure out the right thing to do. I saw both Jake and Mack raise their weapons. This was it. We were going to have to attack or risk being surrounded. I raised my machine-gun, signalled to the others I was ready and ...

Beep, beep, beep, beep ...

Was that an explosive about to detonate? As I opened my eyes and my mind cleared, I realized the noise was coming from my bleeper. I'd been dreaming. I'd fallen asleep in a chair. I couldn't help laughing out loud with relief as I checked my message and switched my bleeper off.

'What's so funny?' asked Jerry, who was reading the message on his own bleeper.

'I was dreaming about our little

adventure in the jungle last summer,' I replied.

'Nothing funny about that trip,' Jerry commented. 'It took months for my poor leg to recover. And even longer for my stomach to get over those maggots we had to eat.'

I groaned at the memory. When people talk about the SAS they generally think that all we do is fight. But no one in the SAS would ever deliberately look for a fight. If they did they would be RTUd (returned to their own unit), which is the worst thing that can happen to an SAS soldier. SAS soldiers will fight when necessary, but their training is really all about survival in extreme situations. We're trained to the limits of physical endurance. Stamina and discipline, both mental and physical, are vital to survival and form an essential part of our training.

Our unit had been tested to the limit on that last jungle mission nine months ago. Me, Jake, Jerry and Mack had been trapped in the heart of the jungle, pursued by terrorists set on killing us. We'd destroyed an old aircraft hangar that had been stacked with their counterfeit money – millions of dollars and pounds sterling, ready to flood the western market. So, naturally, the terrorists were out for revenge. As we were escaping, Jerry had taken a machine-gun burst that had broken his leg. This meant we had to take turns carrying him through the jungle while the other two kept guard, one on point at the front, one at the rear. Our aim was not to stand and fight the terrorists chasing us, but to get to the rendezvous (RV) point where a chopper was supposed to be coming in to pick us up.

Unfortunately for us, everything that could go wrong did go wrong. We lost equipment, ran out of rations and, when we got to the RV point, the chopper wasn't there. It took us another week of travelling through the jungle before we were picked up. We lived off what we could find to eat, including the maggots Jerry had spoken about, and filtered any available water so that it was just about drinkable. It was the ultimate survival test and a real lesson that survival isn't just about being physically tough, it's about mental attitude: the will to survive against all the odds.

'Come on, then,' said Jerry. 'Stop day-dreaming. Didn't you read the bleeper message? There's an urgent briefing in the lecture hall. Top priority.'

We made our way down to the lecture hall and waited for our commanding officer to arrive and fill us in. By 13.00 hours there were twenty of us in the hall, ten from D Squadron, and ten from G Squadron. Everyone else was out on duties, but the word was that they had been recalled and were already on their way to join us. Something very big was up.

The SAS works in teams of four and all my team were present – me, Jake Patterson, Jerry Rudd and 'Mack' McGinniss. At twenty-five years old, Jerry was the eldest. Next came Jake at twenty-three, then Mack, who was twenty-one. Finally there was me, at nineteen the youngest. I was often referred to as 'the baby of the outfit', but I knew it was only a gag and there was no real dig intended. Believe me, the training for the SAS puts years on you, as well as muscle. You may think you're tough and know everything about military life and survival when you start the training. However, after about a week you realize you know nothing. By the second week you've learned about surviving out on the bare mountains overnight in appalling conditions, carrying a full pack weighing twenty-five kilos dead weight, plus your weapon and ammunition. When you finish the three weeks of thirty-mile runs across the Brecon Beacons in Wales, you know you've only just scratched the surface of what training to be a soldier in the SAS is all about.

That's why only about one in ten of the people who apply actually makes it into the SAS. When you've gone through all the training and come out the other side with an SAS badge, you have a common bond with all the other blokes who've also passed – a bond that's unbreakable. In a tight corner every SAS soldier would be prepared to stand by his mates, no matter what. That was how I felt about my squad: they were mates as well as fellow soldiers.

Jake, the shortest of our team at 5 feet 6, had short, cropped, brown hair and a physique like a rugby player, which wasn't surprising, because rugby was his favourite sport. Sometimes we called him 'Eeyore' after that donkey in the Winnie-the-Pooh books, because Jake was inclined to be very negative, saying things like 'This'll never work' and 'This is the worst mess we could be in'.

Jerry, on the other hand, was an eternal optimist. When we'd been in the jungle, hauling him through swamps and over twisted tree roots, every jolt agony for him with his busted leg, he'd just gritted his teeth, forced a laugh and said, 'We'll be all right, fellas.' Jerry originally came from Fiji, in the Pacific. It's often struck me that for such a small island, Fiji has got quite a few soldiers in the SAS. Fijian, English, Scot, New Zealander – it doesn't matter where you come from: in the SAS it's who you are that matters.

Mack was the biggest member of my squad – all 6 foot 2 of him. He was a Scot, with a big bush of red hair hanging over his ears and an enormous walrus moustache that hung over his mouth. When people used to make comments about the size of his moustache, he'd say: 'Yes, but think of the advantages when eating. You people without moustaches only taste soup once. I get tae taste it for hours afterwards!'

The rest of the lads in the lecture hall were a mixed bunch: tall men, short men, big-muscled guys, guys with thin wiry bodies. Some had long hair over their ears; some were shaven-headed. Like I said, there's no one physical type that makes an SAS soldier. Unlike the regular army, who are all stamped to look the same, SAS soldiers are individuals, thinking for themselves, but working together as the tightest team you could ever find anywhere.

Right now we were talking about why we'd all been called in for an urgent briefing. Rumours had been circulating all morning. Again and again the name 'South Carolina' kept cropping up.

'I've heard what's up,' Jake told us confidently. 'The Guantinians have invaded South Carolina. We're going to retake it.'

'South Carolina!' snorted Mack. 'That's nothing to do with us! That's the Americans' problem – let them sort it out.' Then he added wistfully, 'I wouldn't mind a break in the southern states of America.

I've seen all those cowboy films about the Civil War and the scenery looks great.'

'Not that Carolina, you idiot,' said Jake. '*Our* South Carolina.'

Mack looked puzzled.

'I didn't know we had one,' he said.

'This one's in the South Atlantic Ocean,' I said. 'I nearly went there once when I was in the Marines.'

'Nearly?' asked Jake.

I nodded.

'It was too rough to get the ship near enough, so we had to sail past,' I explained. 'The seas can be pretty dangerous down there, especially when winter kicks in.'

'Great,' groaned Jake. 'If we are going down there, it's the wrong time of year.'

He was right. It was April – springtime in the Northern Hemisphere but, down south winter was just starting. Conditions on South Carolina would just be beginning to get nasty.

Just then Sergeant Stevens appeared.

'OK, lads,' he called. 'Take your seats!'

The chatter stopped and we all sat down. Colonel Stannard, our commanding officer, entered.

21

'Right, men,' he said. 'I'll make this as brief as I can. Four days ago a party of scrap metal dealers arrived on the island of South Carolina. For those of you unfamiliar with South Carolina –' and here Jake couldn't resist giving Mack a friendly nudge in the ribs – 'it's on the other side of the world, in the South Atlantic, about a thousand miles north of the Antarctic. It's part of our territories down there called the Lincoln Islands.

'South Carolina is a tiny speck in the freezing ocean far away from the main group of the Lincoln Islands. No one lives there. At least, not permanently. Until Britain stopped its whaling operations in the 1960s, it was a way station for our whaling fleet. Now the British Antarctic Survey organization have been using one of the island's old whaling stations at Solsborg as their base for scientific surveys. It's also one of the main jumping-off points to the South Pole. The other whaling station – twenty miles further along the south coast at a harbour called Troon – has fallen into ruin after being abandoned. Now it's an eyesore of rusting metal waiting to be cleaned up, as those of you who may have done a tour of duty on South Carolina will know.

'After years of wondering what to do about this messy rubbish dump, a contract was finally arranged between the British Government and a firm of scrap-metal dealers in Guantina, on the east coast of South America, and the nearest mainland country to the Lincoln Islands. The dealers were to clear the site at Troon, taking away all the old bits of rusting metal.

'Unfortunately, when the dealers landed at Troon four days ago, they put up the Guantinian flag.'

'Putting up their flag on our territory!' snorted Mack. 'They've got some cheek!'

'Exactly,' nodded Stannard. 'At first, most of the scientists of the British Antarctic Survey team thought it was a joke. However, the leader of the team, Dr Eric Munroe, who also has the official title of Magistrate of South Carolina, didn't think it was so funny. Although South Carolina has been British territory for the last few hundred years, he knew that the Guantinians have been doing their best to stake a claim to it. The scrap-metal dealers putting up their country's flag was a statement to that effect.

'Dr Munroe told the dealers to take the Guantinian flag down. They refused. So he got in touch by radio-telephone with the Governor of the Lincoln Islands in Port Edward. The governor, in turn, telephoned the Foreign Office in London to ask them to get in touch with the Guantinian Government and tell the scrap-metal dealers to take the flag down. The Guantinian Government refused. They even hinted that they were considering sending a force of Marines to "protect the scrap-metal dealers against possible hostile acts by the British on the island".

'As the only British on the island were the Antarctic Survey's eight scientists, who were more interested in collecting data about wildlife, plants and the weather, this all seemed a bit far-fetched. But the Governor of the Lincoln Islands was aware of the danger to the scientists if the Guantinians carried out their threat to send in their Marines. So he decided he had to act to protect the scientists, and also the sovereignty of South Carolina. He sent twelve British Marines, who were carrying out a regular tour of duty in the Lincoln Islands, to South Carolina to police the situation.

'It took the Marines three days to get to South Carolina on an ice-breaker. I tell you this to give you some idea of the conditions out in the South Atlantic at this time of year. Our Marines made their HQ with the scientists at Solsborg. At the same time they set up an observation post near Troon to keep watch on the scrap-metal dealers at the derelict whaling station there.

'Earlier today the Guantinian ice-breaker *Paraiso* entered Troon harbour and put ashore one hundred and fifty Guantinian Marines, loaded to the teeth with weapons and heavy artillery. Along with it came a frigate with another fifty Marines, and more weapons. And not just land weapons: an armed helicopter flew from the *Paraiso* over the island, spotting British positions.

'So, at the moment we have twelve Marines on the island to defend it, but against those odds we don't know how long they can hold out. As we understand it, the Guantinians have got heavy weapons and our Marines have only light ordnance. If our boys can hold out till the end of tomorrow, they will have done very well.'

There was a noticeable silence in the hall. Suddenly no one was making jokes any more. We went cold at the thought of twelve of our boys stuck on an island in the middle of the freezing sea, lightly armed and with only eight scientists for support, under attack by two hundred heavily armed Guantinian Marines.

Stannard let this sink in and then, in a chillingly calm voice, he continued.

'We expect the Guantinian soldiers to force our men to surrender, no matter how much resistance they put up. We have tried radioing through to them, but communications have been difficult. We suspect the Guantinians are deliberately interfering with radio traffic.

'If our men are taken prisoner – and I'd rather that happen than they perish trying to resist – then we have a chance of getting them back alive. With the weather as it is down there, we don't expect the Guantinians to return home with any prisoners immediately. Our guess is that they'll capture our men and keep them on the island, or on board their ships, as a precaution against us mounting a counter-attack.'

'Human shields,' muttered Jerry.

'Exactly,' nodded Stannard. 'We are going to retrieve this situation. We are going to rescue our men and retake the island. It's going to be done in two phases. The first phase will use D Squadron.'

I sat up, alert. D Squadron was my squadron. Me, Jake, Mack, Jerry and a dozen others.

'D Squadron will fly out to Ascension Island tonight, arriving by tomorrow morning,' continued Stannard. 'From there you'll journey by Navy vessel to as near as you can get to South Carolina. Also with you will be a detachment of 42 Commando and another of Royal Marines. They will all stay on board the vessel while D Squadron are helicoptered covertly on to the island. Exact instructions for this insertion, and for the rest of the engagement, will be dispatched to you as you're on your way south.

'Your sea journey will take about a week, depending on the weather in the South Atlantic. There's no quicker way, I'm afraid. Conditions down there now make a parachute drop into the sea or on to land way out of the question.

'SAS G Squadron will follow from England with the rest of the task force that is being assembled. This is going to be a large force, with destroyers, frigates and an aircraft carrier. It will be a combined operation, involving the SAS, SBS, Marines, Army, Navy and Air Force. We're going to throw everything we've got at them. It's going to be a show of muscle, to prove to the Guantinians that we won't be intimidated. When D Squadron retakes South Carolina – as I know you will – it's possible that the Guantinians might mount a counter-offensive to retake it. They might think twice when they learn the size of the force that's heading towards them.

'So, gentlemen, that's it. Our men are in trouble down there. British territory has been stolen. Get it back. Get them back.'

Chapter 2
THE SOUTH ATLANTIC

Twenty-four hours later, the sixteen of us from D Squadron were on HMS *Antrim*, heading south. The flight from Britain to Ascension Island had been long and uncomfortable, as most military flights are. There certainly weren't any air stewardesses serving food or drink, so it was almost a relief to get on to the *Antrim* for the long journey to South Carolina. As Colonel Stannard predicted, it was very slow. In addition to me, Jake, Jerry and Mack, there was Pete Hudson, Marty Nielson, Andy Swan, Zed Zanu, Banco Watts, Dobbs Dobson, Frog French, Mick McNulty, Tony Weathers, Wiggy Jones, Nick Randall, and our commander, Captain Wilson. The sixteen members of D Squadron.

During the week on the *Antrim* we did

our best to keep fit. There wasn't much room below decks to do a proper training run, and the ship rolling badly in the high seas meant it wasn't sensible to run on deck. But we developed a series of exercises, presses and lifts, using whatever we could find as weights, and stuck to it rigidly every day. Being fit and healthy is absolutely essential in the SAS. The stronger your body is, the better it will resist illness and pain and carry you through situations where most people would just crack up, roll over and die.

The rest of the assault squad on board – the fifty Commandos and the sixty or so Royal Marines – seemed a bit amused by all our physical activity. They preferred to keep themselves occupied playing cards or reading. However, some of them joined in a series of four-a-side football games one day. It was a mini-competition: SAS against Marines against Commandos. To our annoyance, the Marines won! Although, as Jerry said, they had an unfair advantage, being used to playing football on a pitch that rolled about most of the time.

As we travelled we listened to the radio,

trying to find out as much as we could about what was happening to our Marines on South Carolina. The Marines did brilliantly, considering the forces against them. Their small arms were useless against heavy artillery and an armed helicopter. Even so, it took three days for the Guantinians to defeat them. They kept on the move, one step ahead of the Guantinian Marines, ambushing them when they could.

Finally, the Guantinians pulled all their troops back to their two ships and sent their helicopter out to identify our Marines' positions. Then they bombarded those positions with heavy 100mm guns. Reports indicated that at least one of our Marines had been wounded. Faced with the prospect of all his men and the scientists being killed – and with no way of fighting that kind of heavy bombardment – the lieutenant commanding the Marines had no choice but to surrender.

We were three days out of Ascension Island when the news of the surrender came through to us on the *Antrim*. The mood of the Marines on board was angry. At the same time, they were proud of how

31

their comrades had resisted so bravely and held out for so long.

'Don't worry,' I said to one of the Marines. 'Once we get there, we'll free them.'

'If you don't, we will,' he replied grimly. 'No Guantino's going to hold my mates prisoner.'

As we neared South Carolina, the weather reports on the radio didn't sound good. We were heading into Arctic conditions. Ice, snow, blizzards. Temperatures of -40°C.

'It's going to be a plank job,' said Mack.

'Planks' were what we called the Army-issue skis.

We were two days away from the island when our orders arrived. When they had been de-coded, they were clear and concise: *SAS D Squadron to gain covert access to island. Disable any enemy helicopter, vehicles and long-range heavy weapons. Free prisoners. When objectives achieved, main force of Commandos and Royal Marines to join SAS and mount assault under cover of fire from naval ship.*

So, as we had always expected, the SAS would be going in first to soften up the enemy. We began to double-check our weapons and equipment. When things go wrong it's often the hardware that lets you down. In the SAS we take every precaution possible to try and make sure that doesn't happen to us.

First, weapons. The SA80 rifle may be standard issue in the British Army but, as far as the SAS are concerned, there's only one rifle and that's the American M16. It's reliable and accurate and operates in all conditions. When you add the standard 203 grenade launcher to the M16, you've got a formidable weapon. Next, the Heckler and Kock sub-machine-gun, the MP5.

Then, plastic explosives, PE4. It's strange stuff. It looks and feels just like white Plasticine and, provided it hasn't got a detonator fixed to it, it's reasonably safe. You must remember to treat it with respect though. If you don't, you could lose an arm. We carry a range of detonators: remote-controlled, electric and the basic sort, which you rig up, fix fuse wire to and then light.

Finally, all the heavy equipment: the pulk (snowsledge), plus two inflatable boats. We'd been studying the map of

South Carolina and noticed loads of inlets and coves. At this time of year they could all be ice, but we couldn't take that chance. Winter was only just starting in the South Atlantic, so the ice could be thin and we'd need a safe way to get across it.

In addition to all the above, we carried abseil ropes made of non-stretch polyester, along with high strength, aluminium karabiners, which we would use to attach ourselves to the ropes. We also had grapnel launchers. These look like a squat shotgun and they use compressed air to launch a grapnel-hook, trailing a climbing rope, to a height of forty-five metres. To fire it, you put it to your shoulder just like a rifle. There were also tents and basic cooking and first-aid equipment, plus ammunition, of course. We'd be on the move in bad weather conditions, so we tried to keep the load to a minimum. However, even with only the bare essentials, there was still a lot to carry with us.

According to our map, there was one inhabited area on South Carolina: the British Antarctic Survey, or BAS, base at the small harbour of Solsborg. It was little more than a cluster of huts with a helicopter landing area. The only other settlement, at Troon, was long gone. However, its harbour could still be used. Both places were now occupied by enemy forces. The Guantinians had taken over the BAS base and moored their two ships in Troon harbour.

A rough track linked Solsborg and Troon, both of which were on the south coast of the island. The rest of South Carolina looked to be a wilderness – empty. Just mountains and bogs.

As the sea journey neared its end, our frustration mounted. We wanted to be in the air, hurtling towards South Carolina at a speed faster than this lumbering ship we were on. But without proper landing strips on the island, the only aircraft that could get us there was a helicopter. We were still too far away to use one: they didn't have the range. Nothing I did seemed to make the time pass any quicker. I marked each day off on a calendar but, as each twenty-four hours passed so incredibly slowly, this just seemed to make things worse. Finally, it was only twenty-four hours to our ETA (estimated time of arrival) and Captain Wilson called us all together for a final briefing.

'OK,' he said, 'we're going to insert ourselves on the island in three Wessex helicopters at dusk tomorrow. We'll land on the coast at the north of the island. We'll make camp for the night, then march across to the enemy position at Solsborg at dawn the next day. The terrain will be difficult, but we don't want to alert them to our presence by landing the choppers too close to them. We want to keep them in the dark that we're on the island until we're ready to strike.'

Wilson tapped the map of the island that he'd tacked to the wall.

'Our latest intelligence report tells us that most of their forces are still at Troon. Their ice-breaker, the *Paraiso*, and their frigate are moored in the harbour there. Our intelligence believes the British prisoners are being held on the *Paraiso*.

'A much smaller force of their Marines is at the BAS base at Solsborg. So, that's why we're going to hit there first. Our aim is not to take Solsborg, at least, not straight away. We hit, and then we withdraw. My hope is that the enemy troops at Solsborg will report to Troon that they're under attack and that Troon will send reinforcements. If I'm right, that will leave Troon exposed, which is our main target. Once there, our first job is to free our men.'

It was early afternoon the next day when we finally sighted South Carolina. D Squadron went up on deck to take a look at our target. Looking through the long-range telescopes, all we could see was a lump of rock sticking out of the sea. Mountains rose up in the middle of it. Clouds hung low around the mountains, obscuring their tops. The ground was a mixture of white, which I took to be snow, and black and grey, which I guessed was rock. Now and then there seemed to be a patch of brown, which might have been scrubland.

'Not much growing there,' muttered Jake beside me, also looking through a telescope.

He was right. There was no sign of any trees. I guessed that the freezing strong winds coming up from the Antarctic would destroy anything trying to grow above a few centimetres.

'It doesn't look worth fighting a war over,' said Mack.

'True,' I replied. 'But then, who'd think a lump of desert with no water and no oil is worth fighting over, but people do. If they didn't, we'd be out of a job.'

As I looked over the sea towards the island, I began to feel I was coming alive again. After those long, mind-numbingly boring days at sea, I was finally going to do what I had been trained for: go into battle. The odds against us were overwhelming – a much larger, heavily armed enemy force, and dangerous and very unpredictable weather conditions. I could feel a sense of excitement rising in me just thinking about it. This was what being in the SAS was all about. We're the best and to me these overwhelming odds just looked like a good challenge.

We went below to make our preparations. We double-checked our weapons and supplies, our clothing and our communications equipment. The pilots of the *Antrim*'s three Wessex helicopters prepared their machines. As daylight

38

began to fade, we took off and headed for that dark and forbidding island.

We were going in.

Chapter 3
ARRIVAL

There were six of us in the back of the Wessex, all fully armed and kitted out for attack. In normal conditions it should have been just a five-minute journey to the land, but these were not normal conditions. A storm had blown up out of nowhere just as we were about to take off. Icy winds hammered us as we lifted into the darkening sky and headed towards the menacing shape of South Carolina. The original plan had been for the pilot to fly just above the sea to escape detection by the enemy's radar on board its frigate. But as the wind whipped the waves up into moving mountains of water, the pilot took the Wessex up higher. We'd have to take our chances with the radar.

The freezing wind howled, although I could barely hear it above the screech of whirling rotor blades as the pilot fought to control the Wessex. The whole helicopter shook violently. Suddenly it plunged down towards the churning sea below, dropping like a stone. I shut my eyes tightly and hung on for dear life, silently praying that the pilot knew what he was doing. It was a few heart-stopping seconds before the helicopter lurched back up into the air, still rocking from side to side. If the engines packed up we'd hit the raging South Atlantic below and disappear beneath the water in seconds. And there'd be no rescue, not in these icy seas. We'd all die. It was that simple.

Alongside us, also fighting the vicious gale-force winds, the other two Wessex choppers were having the same problems we were. Through the open door I could see the ice and snow on South Carolina gleaming white in the evening gloom. Again our pilot fought to control the bucking machine, battling against the elements all the time. He turned the helicopter into the wind and began his descent towards the island. Sleet had sprung up; hard, pointed shards of frozen rain that battered the helicopter like a shower of nails, smashing against the cockpit windscreen, obscuring the pilot's vision. Even with the wipers on, vision was very poor.

'It's like being on a bucking bronco at a rodeo,' muttered Jake sitting beside me, his grip on a handrail tightening to hold himself steady.

'When did you ever ride a bucking bronco at a rodeo?' I asked.

'OK, so I'm using my imagination,' he answered. 'Anyway, I've seen them do it in cowboy films, so I know what it's like. Exactly like being thrown about like this.'

'But if you fall off, you don't drop into a freezing ocean and drown,' I pointed out.

The pilot dropped the Wessex low, hanging over the sea, just above the tops of the white breakers near the shore. The huge waves, driven by the powerful winds, leapt up towards us as they crashed against the dark rocks that surrounded the island. We shuddered from side to side, with wild foaming water hurling up at us from all directions.

Through the door, I could just about see

our target through the driving sleet – a roughly flattened patch of scrub and rock covered with snow.

'Here we go!' announced the pilot. 'Going down!'

As the helicopter came in to land, it was tugged violently to one side by a particularly powerful gust of wind. For a second I thought the pilot had lost it and we were going to topple over. But then I realized we were down. He'd made it.

'Go!'

I leapt out of the Wessex along with Jake, Captain Wilson and the other three, hauling our bergens and equipment along with us. We ran straight for the nearest cover – a small group of rocks – crouching low as we went. Jake and I dragged the pulk between us. I saw the other two helicopters land near by and the rest of our squadron poured out to join us. As the last man hit the ground, the three choppers rose up one by one and headed back towards the *Antrim*.

'So far, so good,' Jake whispered to me. 'At least we're here safely.'

'Let's hope the enemy don't know that,' I replied.

As I watched the helicopters disappearing into the gloom, I strained my ears for any sound that might indicate whether the Guantinians were on their way. Had they picked up our helicopters on their ship's radar? If they had, we had to hope that they would think it was just a reconnaissance mission. Would they send one of their own helicopters to recce? Probably not in this weather. Even so, the sooner we got ourselves under cover the better.

We were all dressed in white Arctic camouflage gear, which suited the conditions on South Carolina. The winds were whipping up into a blizzard of snow and ice. It crossed my mind that if it continued, the helicopters would have difficulty getting back to us if we got into trouble and needed to get off the island quickly. Effectively, we were stuck there with no way back. I remembered something I'd read in a book about the Vikings. When they arrived somewhere, they burnt their boats so that they couldn't get away. Because Vikings didn't surrender, it left them with two choices – victory or death. It felt a bit like that for me right then.

We posted four men as look-outs. The

rest of us got to work, building a temporary shelter in the lee of the cluster of rocks, using the sledge and the two-man tents. In these conditions it was hard work and, despite the freezing cold, I was soon sweating inside my gear. Even with our look-outs on watch, I kept my eyes and ears alert for any sign of enemy activity, scanning the night sky for approaching lights. Either we'd been lucky and they didn't know we were here, or the enemy had decided the weather was too bad to venture out.

Once the shelter was up, Jerry got on the radio and reported back to the *Antrim* that we had secured our position. From now on there'd be no further radio communications with the *Antrim* until we'd made things ready for 42 Commando and the Marines to join us on the island. Or, if we took such heavy losses that we had to be evacuated. As far as I was concerned, evacuation wasn't an option. We were the SAS. Our mission was to rescue the hostages and that was exactly what we were going to do.

We were on our own. Sixteen against two hundred.

Chapter 4
A FREEZING HELL

That night we worked in shifts to keep look-out. Me, Jake, Jerry and Mack took look-out duty together, each covering a different direction: north, south, east, west. Not that there was much visibility. The blizzard seemed to get worse as the night wore on, driving ice and snow into my eyes as I scanned the dark landscape. Even the lenses of our night glasses iced over straight away. We had landed in a freezing hell.

As dawn arrived, I saw that our position had been completely hidden by the blizzard. Thick layers of snow had formed against the sledge and the tents, turning them into a mini-mountain against the cluster of rocks. This was a stroke of luck for us because, just after dawn, I heard a helicopter approaching. I knew from the sound of its engine that it wasn't one of ours. It was an Alouette. The Guantinians were approaching.

We kept under cover as the helicopter flew over our position, then circled, before flying off.

'We should have brought it down,' said Mack.

'No sense in alerting them we're here, just yet,' I replied. 'If they haven't spotted us, all well and good.'

We scanned the skies for any signs of the Alouette helicopter returning. When we were sure the coast was clear, we loaded our heavy equipment on to the sledge. It was, as Mack had correctly forecast, a 'plank' job. We all put on our skis before setting off across the icy landscape. We divided into four teams and took turns in pulling the pulk. With the machine-gun, missile-launcher, ammunition and explosives, it weighed 110 kilos. Our own bergens weighed forty-five kilos, so it was hard work, carrying and hauling so much weight across the rough terrain.

As we got further inland, our progress became more difficult because the ground kept changing. For some stretches it was all snow. Then suddenly the snow would clear and it would be bare scrub and rock. No sooner had we taken our skis off, when we'd run into more snow and have to put them on again. It was all very time-consuming and frustrating.

It took ten tough hours of walking, skiing and hauling before we came within sight of the BAS base at Solsborg. Immediately, we dropped down into prone positions, pressing ourselves into the soft covering of snow on the ice and rocks. If we could see the Guantinians, then they could see us.

'Right, Rob and Jerry, you're the recce team,' said Captain Wilson. 'Get as close as you can and report back.'

Jerry and I nodded. We took off our skis and ran a radio-check to make sure the radios and microphones in our helmets were working properly. Then we set off, crawling on all fours.

Ahead of us, about a 100 metres away from the perimeter of the compound of huts, was a low ridge of ice that the wind had built up. We worked our way towards this ice-ridge as fast as we could on our elbows and knees, our rifles held just above the snow. A couple of times I sank as the snow gave way, but I hauled myself out and struggled on. Finally we made it to the ice-ridge. It was the height of a low wall. Perfect cover. There, just in front of us, were the huts that made up the British Antarctic Survey base. A Guantinian flag was flying from the flag-pole.

Not for much longer, I thought to myself.

The Alouette helicopter was parked on the rough landing pad by the side of the huts. Near by was one of the BAS's All-terrain vehicles (ATVs).

'What have you got?' came the voice of Captain Wilson through the headphones in my helmet.

'Four huts. One ATV. One Alouette chopper,' I whispered into my microphone. 'No one outside keeping watch. Very sloppy, or they obviously don't know yet that we're on the island.'

'How many personnel?'

'Just counting,' I replied.

I trained my binoculars on the windows of the nearest hut.

'Looks like at least six of them in the hut with the brown door,' I answered. 'No ... wait. Seven. At least seven, but there could be others I can't see. From the size of the hut, I'd guess a dozen in total. What about you, Jerry?'

Jerry had focused his binoculars on another hut, and he nodded. 'About the same. I can see five men moving about at one end. At least two at the other end – can't see through that window very clearly. I'm guessing the same as Rob: a dozen men in each hut.'

'OK,' said Wilson. 'Jake and Mack are coming to join you. Need them to bring anything?'

I looked at Jerry and we grinned as the same thought struck us.

'Something to take out the chopper and the ATV would be handy,' I said.

Jerry nodded.

'There mightn't be a better opportunity than this,' he added. 'Take those out and they're going to find travelling difficult. Certainly, if we take out the chopper one of their links with the ship will be cut.'

'Done,' said Wilson. 'They're on their way. Out.'

Jerry and I put our binoculars back to our eyes and kept them trained on the huts, watching for any signs of enemy movement. The door of one of the huts opened and a soldier appeared in the doorway. He was dressed in Arctic gear, a parka and heavy boots, but there was no sign of him carrying any weapon.

'Let's hope he's not the chopper pilot,' whispered Jerry. 'I'm not letting this opportunity go.'

He brought his rifle to bear on the soldier.

The soldier headed along the walkway between the huts to enter what I knew from the plan of the base was the toilet and shower block.

'He's going to the loo,' I said.

Jerry lowered his rifle.

'He's a lucky man,' he said.

We heard a noise behind us and turned to see Jake and Mack crawling towards our position on their hands and knees. Jake was carrying a large bag slung over his shoulder. They joined us behind the ice-ridge. We gestured to them to keep their voices low.

'Someone's out in the compound,' I whispered, gesturing towards the base.

'Toilet call,' added Jerry. 'When he's back in his hut, we can do the business.'

'What have you got?' I asked.

'Plastic. Detonators – instant, timer and remote. We weren't sure what you wanted, so we brought them all,' said Jake.

'Three remotes,' I said. 'Two for the chopper, one for the ATV. I'll take the Alouette if you take the ATV. Jerry keeps watch.'

'Fine by me,' said Jake.

Jake and I began to share out the plastic explosive, putting it into our shoulder bags, along with the pencil-thin detonators.

'Are you guys planning on detonating it yourselves, or do you want me to set them off?' asked Mack.

'You'd better do it,' I said. 'Just in case anything should happen to us out there.'

'I hear you,' said Mack, setting the correct frequency on the remote controls to link them with the detonators. 'Leave it to me.'

'And no setting them off too soon,' I warned him. 'Not like the last time ...'

Mack grinned. Last year we'd been on an operation together in a desert country. Our mission was to sabotage a mobile weapons launcher. I'd fixed the plastic explosives to the launcher and had barely got a few metres away, when Mack had set it off.

'I had no choice,' Mack chuckled. 'Remember, I told you then: they'd spotted you and they were going to kill you and disable the plastic. I saved your life.'

'You nearly *ended* it,' I said.

'Trust me,' said Mack. 'I know what I'm doing.'

'Our man's coming out,' interrupted Jerry, who had been watching the toilet and shower block through his binoculars. 'He's heading back to his hut.'

I also trained my binoculars on the soldier. We watched as he went into his hut and shut the door.

'Right,' I said. 'Let's hope no one else feels the need to go to the loo in the next few minutes. Ready, Jake? Jerry?'

They both nodded.

'Let's do it,' said Jake.

The three of us crawled along behind the ice-ridge, carefully cradling our rifles and the bags containing the explosive as we moved. Behind us, Mack took up his position behind the ridge, training his rifle on the compound, ready to give us covering fire if we needed it.

Jake, Jerry and I travelled about a 100 metres behind the ridge until we were out of sight of the huts' windows and only fifty metres from the helicopter and the ATV.

We pulled ourselves up over the ridge and dropped into the snow on the other side. Here it was so thin that scrub and rock poked through.

'No sense crawling over this lot,' muttered Jerry.

I nodded.

'Let's go,' I said.

Crouching low, the three of us ran at speed, covering the distance to the Alouette and the ATV as quickly as possible. As we neared the helicopter I was already opening my bag with one hand and taking out the plastic explosive. While Jerry dropped to a firing position behind the helicopter, his gun trained on the huts, I set to work.

I packed some of the explosive at the rear of the chopper, just by the tail rotor. When I was sure it was fixed securely, I pushed the remote-controlled detonator into the mass of plastic. Then I moved to the belly of the Alouette, underneath where the fuel tank would be. Once more I moulded the plastic explosive into shape, packed it against the fuselage and pushed the thin detonator into it. I shot a quick glance across to the ATV. I saw Jake hauling himself out from beneath it. He gave a thumbs up.

'Right,' I hissed at Jerry. 'That's it. We're go.'

Jerry nodded and we all turned to head back towards the ice-ridge. Just then, I heard a door slam open.

Immediately, we threw ourselves flat on the ground, turning as we did so towards the sound, hoping we hadn't been seen.

We had.

There was a shout of 'Atacar!', Spanish for 'Attack!'. Next a Guantinian soldier opened up from the open door. Bullets smacked into the ground near us, throwing chips of rocks and ice up into our faces.

Don't let them hit the explosives! I prayed silently.

Jerry let off a burst from his rifle towards the enemy soldier, and we heard the door slam shut.

Looking towards the huts, I saw that windows were being opened and rifle-barrels were being poked through them.

'Time to go!' said Jerry.

He fired one last burst. Jake and I did the same and then we ran zigzag fashion towards the ice-ridge, bullets flying all around us, even plucking at our clothes.

BRR-BRRR-BRRR!!!!!

Mack opened fire from his position behind the ridge. There was the sound of glass shattering as he shot out windows in the huts. The enemy soldiers stopped firing and they ducked away from the windows, giving me, Jake and Jerry time to complete our dash to the ridge and hurl ourselves over it.

'OK!' I shouted at Mack. 'Blow the plastic!'

'You're sure you're not still too close to it?' laughed Mack.

'Just blow it!' I yelled.

'After all, I suppose they know we're here now!' grinned Jerry.

The air was filled with the roar of explosions – two from the heli-pad, one from the ATV. Jake had set his plastic explosives underneath the traction mechanism on the ATV. As Mack detonated it, the caterpillar tracks were blown out, curling up like broken elastic-bands, with bits of metal flying everywhere.

On the helicopter, the explosive at the tail end blew off the rear rotor. But the explosion of the fuel tank was truely spectacular. It was so huge that for a second I thought we were going to be engulfed in it. There was a massive WHOOOMPPP!! and a ball of red and white flame shot out from the chopper. Then it seemed to rise up into the air as the fuel tank went up. As it crashed down it began to crumple and fall apart in a tangle of twisted metal and thick black oily smoke.

Mack kept up sporadic firing at the huts to keep the Guantinians at bay while we ran along behind the ice-ridge, crouching low.

'One to us,' I said. 'Well done, Mack.'

From the huts came a burst of gunfire as someone braved Mack's fire. The bullets skimmed through the air just above our heads.

'Time to go,' said Jerry.

'We're still carrying plastic explosive in this bag,' said Mack. 'I don't fancy being around if one of them hits that.'

'Let's give them something to think about,' said Jake.

He pulled out a grenade, took out the pin, then tossed it towards the hut where the firing was coming from. The grenade rolled to a stop just beneath an open window.

'When that goes off, with luck they'll think we're firing mortars at them and get away from the windows.'

The gunfire continued. We counted down. 6 ... 5 ... 4 ... 3 ... 2 ... 1 ...

Boooooom!!!

As the grenade went off, the firing stopped abruptly.

'Let's go!' snapped Mack.

We were already running, hauling our weapons and bags with us. Every few steps two of us turned and fired off a burst towards the huts, covering the other pair as they ran on ahead. Soon the four of us were out of range of the enemy's small-arms weapons. If they wanted to chase us with bigger weapons, they'd have to come out of the huts to do it.

We regrouped with the rest of the squad.

'Mission accomplished,' I said to Captain Wilson. 'The chopper and the ATV both out of action.'

'And pretty thoroughly, by the sound of

it!' grinned Wilson. 'Good job. Right, my guess is that all that action will have the Guantinians at Solsborg bleating for help from the major force on their ships docked at Troon.'

'Do you think they'll move the ship along the coast to Solsborg?' I asked.

Wilson mulled it over.

'They might send the frigate, but I doubt if they'll move the ice-breaker,' he said at last. 'It secures the base at Troon. Remember, there's no base for them ashore and no proper cover. So the ice-breaker is probably their HQ. I think they'll send major reinforcements overland to Solsborg – with ATVs, heavy weapons, the lot. And on the way they'll be looking for us. If I'm right, it's a good opportunity to free the prisoners on the ice-breaker, if that's where they are.'

'And if you're wrong?' queried Jake.

Wilson grinned.

'We'll end up in big trouble. Really big trouble,' he said.

Chapter 5
HUNTED MEN

We now had to decide our next move. There were a couple of options available, neither of them easy. The distance from Solsborg to Troon was twenty miles, along a rough track. If Captain Wilson was right, the reinforcements from Troon would soon be using that track. Our first option was to avoid this enemy force and travel away from the track over the uneven terrain.

The second option was to engage the enemy by laying an ambush along the track. This option wasn't favoured, because it would mean facing overwhelming odds in a face-to-face situation. It would also place the enemy between us and the ice-breaker at Troon, and it was the ice-breaker that was our next target. If our men were being kept prisoner on it, as our intelligence suspected, we wanted to free them. If the prisoners weren't on it, taking over the ice-breaker would still put us in a powerful position.

'Looks like we're taking the hard route again then, lads,' commented Mack, as we checked our equipment before setting off north-eastwards, away from the track. The plan was to change direction after two miles and head due east, staying parallel to the track, but at a distance of about two miles. Near enough to keep watch on the track and any enemy movements, but far enough away – we hoped – to avoid being spotted. Then we'd drop south to the harbour at Troon. This detour would add some four or five miles, depending on the terrain, meaning a journey of some twenty-five-plus miles. We hoped it would be worth it.

We didn't know whether the enemy had sent a force after us from Solsborg. For all we knew, they could be hot on our tail even now. However, Captain Wilson suspected the Guantianians at Solsborg would decide to sit tight and wait for reinforcements from Troon. But those reinforcements could be scouring the island, looking for us. We were now hunted men.

*

The rough country we were crossing made travelling frustrating and exhausting. The worst thing was the snow – you never knew what it might be hiding. There were frozen swamps and deep crevasses all over the island. We had to take great care – not easy when you're being hunted by a trigger-happy enemy and so have to move as quickly as possible.

On board the *Antrim* we'd studied maps of South Carolina. Not just Ordnance Survey ones, but the geological maps that the British Antarctic Survey had produced. These showed the different sorts of rock strata and soil in each part of the island. From these maps we could work out roughly where the snow might be fairly safe to travel over, and where it might be hiding something.

The type of snow varied. Sometimes it was so soft and powdery that you sank into it, even on skis. In other places it had such a high ice content and was so firm that you could drive a tank over it. So far our judgement had been correct and we'd stuck to snow that was frozen enough to support our weight on skis, even when we were pulling our equipment on the pulk.

We'd travelled about eight miles when we heard the sound of some ATVs on the track between Troon and Solsborg. Immediately we took cover, flattening ourselves into the snow.

I pulled out my binoculars to study the track. There were four ATVs travelling along it in covoy. Behind each was an open truck, with chains round its tyres to cope with the ice and snow on the track. One of the middle trucks was loaded with artillery equipment: missile launchers, semi-heavy guns. The other three trucks were full of soldiers, all wearing parkas pulled over their heads and with their rifles held ready for use.

'Look at them. They haven't seen us,' whispered Jake. 'We could hit them right now, take them all out.'

'We could take out some of them,' I agreed. 'But then we'd be into a running battle, and that's not our mission right now.'

'True,' sighed Jake wistfully.

As the convoy trundled past, I started to do a head count. Each truck held sixteen soldiers. Three sixteens were forty-eight. Each ATV looked as it if held another ten soldiers. Four ATVs meant another forty enemy soldiers: ninety-eight soldiers all together. In round figures, 100. We'd calculated there were about fifty men stationed at Solsborg. Our intelligence said that the enemy had a total strength of 200 on the island. That meant there would be about fifty men left guarding the *Paraiso* ice-breaker at Troon. Or out looking for us.

We waited silently until the convoy had gone past, and then we got to our feet, back on to our skis.

'I'm guessing there were a hundred men in that convoy,' said Captain Wilson. 'Anyone work out anything different?'

We all shook our heads. Each one of us had reached the same conclusion.

'Right, let's get on,' said Wilson. 'But keep your eyes and ears alert. There may be another convoy. Or the Guantinos may have soldiers searching for us.'

We set off again, pushing our way along the hard-packed snow on our skis, rifles slung around our shoulders, ready-to-hand if needed. Every sense was alert – eyes scanning the landscape; ears listening to every sound; noses sniffing the air for any tell-tale smells of man or machine. A hint of diesel fumes on the wind could mean a vehicle approaching. All the time, we made sure that when we came to open ground we moved across it quickly, getting to potential cover fast. We assumed we were being hunted, so we used every skill to make sure we survived.

About four miles from Troon, Mack and I were hauling the pulk, making good progress over the smooth snow. Ahead of us, Dobbs was on point, skiing smoothly, rifle cradled in his arms.

Without warning, the snow opened up beneath him and he disappeared.

Chapter 6
CREVASSE DANGER

'Halt!' I yelled.

Mack and I brought the pulk to an abrupt stop near the hole made by Dobbs.

I held up my hand to warn the rest of the men following of the danger. Captain Wilson and Pete approached the hole carefully, testing the snow with their ski poles before they moved, until they were at the edge of the hole. I left Mack with the pulk and moved over to join them.

We looked into the jagged hole – a crevasse hidden by the snow. There was no sign of Dobbs, just a mound of fallen snow at the bottom of the crevasse, about six metres down. As we watched, the mound began to move and Dobbs's head poked out.

'Are you all right?' asked Wilson. 'Any injuries?'

'I think I've put my left shoulder out,' grimaced Dobbs.

'I'll go down,' I volunteered.

The other guys, as always, had been thinking and planning ahead. Already Wiggy and Nick had tied one end of a rope to an outcrop of rock near by. They brought the free end over and dropped it into the crevasse.

I looped the rope through a karabiner, hooked it on to my belt, and began to descend the rope into the crevasse. Down at the bottom, Dobbs had wriggled his way out of the snowfall that had covered him. I could tell he was in pain by the expression on his face. I checked his left shoulder.

'It's dislocated all right,' I said. 'I'm going to put it back. Yell if it hurts.'

'If you hurt me I'll do better than that: I'll punch you in the face!' said Dobbs, doing his best to make a joke if it.

Putting a dislocated shoulder back into the joint isn't easy, especially on a pile of snow at the bottom of a crevasse.

Dobbs lay down on the snow. I sat next him, took hold of his left wrist in both my hands and put my right foot into his armpit.

'OK,' I said. 'Try and think of something else.'

'Like what –?' Dobbs began, and at that moment I pulled on his arm.

A look of pain crossed Dobbs's face and he gritted his teeth, but at the same time I heard the tell-tale 'click' as his arm went back into his shoulder joint.

I felt movement above me as Nick and Wiggy came down the rope.

'How is he?' asked Wiggy.

'Perfectly able to talk for myself, thank you,' grunted Dobbs.

Dobbs had got up and was flexing the fingers of his left hand and bending his elbow, getting movement back into his arm.

'Thanks, Rob,' he said.

'Don't mention it,' I replied. 'I'll send you my doctor's bill later.'

'Are you lot going to stay down there, chattering?' demanded a voice from above us.

I looked up. It was Captain Wilson, looking down.

'If everything's OK, let's get you all back up here,' he said. 'In case you've forgotten, there's a war on ...'

'On our way, Cap,' I said.

Wiggy and Nick took off Dobbs's skis and started to fix a harness on to him to haul him up, but he shrugged them off.

'I can do it,' he said.

'You could put your shoulder out again,' pointed out Nick.

'When I want nursemaiding I'll let you know,' said Dobbs.

Nick shrugged.

Dobbs hauled himself up the rope, using his feet and his good arm. We followed, bringing his skis up with us.

'OK,' said Captain Wilson. 'Let's move. From now on, whoever's on point, watch out for cracks in the snow that could be crevasses.'

There were no more major incidents after that. No more Guantinian soldiers, no more concealed crevasses. Finally, we arrived near Troon.

We took up a position two miles away and studied it through our binoculars. At first sight the old whaling station looked just a wreck of fallen-down, rotting wooden huts with collapsed corrugated-iron roofs. Mangled machinery lay broken everywhere. Rusty wire cables formed orange lines into the snow between it. The place looked exactly what it was: a scrap yard filled with the leftover junk of an industry that had died long ago. Then I moved my binoculars and saw the end of a machine-gun, half hidden. There was more than junk here ...

'Two machine-gun posts,' I whispered. 'One behind that old crane. The other inside that fallen down hut near it.'

'Three,' corrected Mack. 'There's another one behind those sheets of corrugated iron.'

I looked again. This time I saw the barrel of the machine-gun poking between two of the metal sheets.

'Got it,' I said.

'They may not be manned,' suggested Jerry. 'They may be there to fool us.'

As he spoke, I spotted a movement from the machine-gun in the old hut. The gun went up, back down and then steadied. It wasn't movement caused by the wind.

'There's certainly someone behind the machine-gun in the old hut,' I said.

I trained my binoculars on the ship in the harbour. The harbour wall was crumbling, but sections of it were still firm enough for a ship to moor alongside. It was the ice-breaker, the *Paraiso*. There was no sign of the frigate. It looked as if Captain Wilson had guessed correctly: it had sailed along the coast to support the enemy at Solsborg. From just off the coast, it could use its guns to bombard inland positions. If we'd stayed at Solsborg, we'd have been caught in its range.

'OK, summing up. At least three machine-gun posts. Possibly more that we haven't been able to see. No other signs of movement, which suggests everyone else is on board the ice-breaker. How do we get past the machine-gun positions and on to the ship without being seen?'

'Wait till nightfall,' suggested Pete. 'Creep in. Take out the machine-gun posts.'

Marty shook his head.

'They'll have lights,' he said. 'If you take a look you can see electric cables. New ones. That means lights working off generators. The harbour will be lit up come nightfall.'

'I still think nightfall will give us our best chance,' said Captain Wilson.

'We could do it by sea,' I suggested.

71

The others turned and looked at me, intrigued.

'We've got the two inflatable rafts,' I reminded them. 'Put four men in each, plus two to paddle back after the others have boarded. We come up on the ship on the open-sea side. The eight get on board the ship and locate the prisoners. Once that's done, they'll signal to those left on land to attack the machine-gun posts. This will keep the gunners occupied while the others get off the ship with the prisoners.'

'So we should end up securing both the ice-breaker and the harbour,' murmured CaptainWilson thoughtfully. He nodded. 'I like it. Volunteers to go in the boats?'

'Me for one,' I said quickly. 'It was my idea.'

'Absolutely,' nodded Wilson. 'You and the rest of your troop in one boat. Pete, you and your troop in the other. OK?'

And so it was agreed. Me, Jake, Jerry and Mack in one boat, with Banco and Wiggy to paddle it back; and Pete, Marty, Andy and Zed as the boarding party in the other boat, with Frog and Mick to bring it back.

'That water will be freezing!' complained Jake. 'Worse than freezing! If we even touch it our hands will turn to solid ice and break off.'

'Then better make sure we don't fall in,' I laughed.

'Joking aside, lads, this is not going to be easy,' said Captain Wilson. 'We have to work together and stay focused. My bet is that the prisoners are on that ship – and their lives depend on this plan working.'

As his words sunk in, I realized that all our lives – including mine and my best mates' – depended on my idea working.

Chapter 7
NIGHT ATTACK

We waited until nightfall before launching from a cove about half a mile along the shore from Troon. The two inflatables slid into the icy water. Two of us held them while the others loaded the equipment – grapnels and launchers, guns, ammunition, and explosives in case we needed to blow open doors on the ship.

We set out along the coast, paddling in unison, keeping the boats abreast of each other. It was an incoming tide, which made life difficult for us at first, each wave pushing the boats back in to the shore. We dug our paddles deep into the water and worked harder, getting a rhythm going. Soon we were out on the open sea. The plan was to use the tide to bring us in to the seawards side of the *Paraiso* and let it hold us against the ship while we climbed on board. If the tide had been going out it would have been much, much harder. We would have needed to find something to tie our inflatable to while we boarded – just Banco and Wiggy paddling against the tide wouldn't have been enough to hold it steady.

We fought the tide to take us almost a mile off shore. I knew that if anything went wrong – for example, if the inflatable sprang a leak and started sinking – we'd be dead within minutes because of the icy temperature of the water. We paddled until we were parallel with the large ice-breaker. Then we began to work our way in towards it, using our paddles as brakes against the tide to slow us down.

'Let's hope no one on board's keeping watch this way,' whispered Jake.

'We'll soon know if they are,' I muttered back.

I kept my eyes on the handrails round the deck. All it needed was for someone to glance in our direction and we'd be dead. Their guns would open up on us and the inflatable would go down, with us in it. We'd either be shot, or drowned, or freeze to death.

Luckily, the Guantinos had decided to stay below decks. We brought our inflatable in near the bows of the *Paraiso*, while Pete and his unit made for the middle. While the other guys paddled to hold our inflatable as steady as they could in the choppy seas, I took out our grapnel and aimed at the handrail about fifteen metres above me. I'd already tied cloth round the metal hook in an attempt to deaden the sound of it catching on the metal handrail.

'Get it right,' whispered Jerry. 'We don't want it scraping down the hull. The Guantinos would be bound to hear that.'

'Worse,' muttered Jake. 'It could come back down on us.'

'Don't worry, I'll get it in one,' I reassured them.

Although I said it with confidence, I didn't feel so sure. Firing a grappling hook upwards while you're standing on solid ground is one thing; trying to keep your balance in an inflatable that's lurching about is a harder task altogether. Jerry and Jake were right: if I missed, we could be in big trouble. We'd either have the Guantinians rushing out to see what the noise was, or we could have a big metal hook coming back down on to our boat and sinking it – or even injuring one of us.

I put the butt of the grapnel-launcher to my shoulder and took aim. I was just about to fire, when a large wave swept in. The inflatable rolled and I slipped. Dobbs grabbed me, just managing to stop me falling over the side into the sea.

'Stop messing about, Rob!' whispered Jake. 'Do it!'

I stumbled back to my feet and looked towards the other inflatable. Pete was having the same trouble, trying to keep his balance so that he could fire his grappling hook.

'You and your great ideas!' snorted Jerry in a whisper.

Once again I steadied myself, the launcher firmly butted into my shoulder. I fired. I felt the recoil as the grapnel hook hurtled skywards. Then it fell over the handrail, out of sight.

I pulled on the rope and felt the claws of the hook grip and hold firm. Quietly I breathed a sigh of relief. Pete had managed to get the same firm grip with his hook. He looked across at me and gave me a thumbs up.

'That's it,' I said. 'Up we go!'

I picked up my rifle, looped it around my shoulder and began the climb, hand over hand on the rope, foot over foot on the side of the ship, as silently as I could.

At the top I clambered over the handrail on to the deck. I crouched down, rifle level, swinging it in an arc, ready to fire if anyone came at me. No one did. Everyone was below decks.

I checked that the claws of the grappling hook were secure before giving a thumbs up to the guys waiting down in the inflatable. One by one they hauled themselves up the rope: Jerry, Jake, Mack. Meanwhile Pete, Marty, Andy and Zed climbed the rope at the middle of the ship. I hauled our rope up, wrapped it round the grappling hook and stowed it out of sight behind a nearby lifeboat. Pete did the same. We didn't want some sailor accidentally coming across the hooks and ropes still fixed to the handrails and raising the alarm.

We stayed there for a moment, crouched behind the deck housing, listening for anyone approaching. Nothing. I heard a radio playing music. It was a muffled sound, coming from somewhere below decks. Sailors relaxing. It looked like we'd been successful: they were completely unaware of our presence. So far, things were going to plan.

On our journey from Ascension Island we had studied plans of the *Paraiso* obtained by intelligence, so we knew its layout.

'You four take the bridge,' suggested Pete. 'We'll find the prisoners.'

'Got it,' I nodded.

While Pete, Marty, Andy and Zed headed for a gangway down below decks, me, Jerry, Jake and Mack went to the bridge, the heart of the ship, its crew's HQ.

Moving through the darkness as quietly as we could, we worked our way along the deck, dodging in and out of every shadow: doorways, deck housing, lifeboats, anything that could be used as cover to hide our approach. Finally, we came to the flight of metal stairs up to the bridge. There was no other way to it.

I crept forwards to the bottom step, and then I began to crawl slowly up the stairs, keeping myself as low as possible. At the top was a door with a glass panel in – the door to the ship's bridge. Mack, Jerry and Jake were close behind me.

I got to the landing at the top of the stairs and crouched down, keeping my head below the level of the glass panel. I looked behind me to make sure the others were in position. Mack, nearest to me, gave me a thumbs up.

I reached up, grabbed the door handle firmly but quietly, and ever so slowly turned it. Kicking a door in for a surprise attack has to be done carefully when you're balancing on a narrow metal grille with a steep flight of steps behind you.

OK. This was it. I stood up, threw open the door and burst on to the bridge, sweeping my rifle from side to side, but held firm in my hands, moving forwards to make room for Mack, Jerry and Jake to rush in after me.

There is something heart-stoppingly frightening about having a door burst open and four men rush in, dressed from head to foot in black, holding automatic rifles, and wearing ammunition all over them.

There is immediate shock and then, as it wears off, complete fear as a person realizes they are staring down the barrel of a rifle that could cut them in two and there is a finger poised on its trigger.

'*Dios!*' exclaimed the man nearest the helm, his mouth dropping open. Good God!

'No, *Británico*,' I responded.

There were five of them on duty. By the look of them, being on watch was a pretty relaxed affair. In Spanish I snapped at them to put their hands up. All SAS troops are encouraged to become fluent in another language. More than one, if possible. As we seemed to spend a lot of time in desert countries, many of the guys had chosen some of the Arabic languages. Banco had even chosen Chinese. Me, I'd stuck to European languages, French and Spanish, which was lucky right now.

While me and Jake kept our guns trained on the sailors, Jerry and Mack tied them up, gagged them, and sat them down on the floor of the bridge.

'They're not military,' commented Jake.

I nodded. The men were not in uniform.

The *Paraiso* was obviously a civilian vessel that had been commandeered by the Guantinian Navy. The only military personnel on board would be the Guantinian Marines left to guard it.

'Jerry and Mack, you stay here,' I said. 'Me and Jake will see how Pete and the others are getting on, and if they need our help.'

Jake and I hurried down the steps, still doing our best to keep our presence a secret for as long as possible. We didn't want to alert the soldiers at the machine-gun posts on the land until we were ready for them.

As we made our way along the deck, I heard the hammering sound of gunfire from one of the gangways that went below, followed by shouting in Spanish and then more gunfire.

'They're in trouble!' shouted Jake, and he hurried down the gangway, rifle levelled.

From the shore I heard frantic shouting from the machine-gun posts. In Spanish the gunners were demanding 'What's going on?' and 'Are we being attacked?'

I rushed into in the shadow of a lifeboat

so that the machine-gunners couldn't see me, and shouted down in Spanish, 'It's all right. Some fool had too much to drink and is letting off his gun. No trouble. Just keep watch. It'll be sorted out!'

The soldiers accepted this explanation, although I could hear unhappy mutterings, mainly about drunken civilian sailors.

From down below I heard another burst of gunfire, more yelling, and then silence.

I moved towards the gangway, rifle held ready, eyes and ears alert. What had happened? Had the Guantinian Marines caught Pete and the others? If so, I'd have expected to hear a lot more shouting and the sound of heavy boots running around. But there was nothing.

I was starting down the gangway when I heard footsteps heading towards it. I swung my rifle barrel down, my finger resting on the trigger.

As I was about to fire, Marty came into view.

'It's OK!' he hissed. 'It's all under control.'

'It didn't sound like it,' I said as I came down the stairs to join him.

'Just a couple of Marines who decided to

put up a fight,' explained Marty. 'We dealt with them. The others are all merchant sailors. Non-combat. One look at us and their hands went up like they were about to sing "Hallelujah".'

I nodded.

'It was the same for us on the bridge,' I told him. 'What about the prisoners?'

'Pete's getting one of the Guantinians to show us where they are, right now.' Marty gestured towards the shore. 'What about the boys on the machine-guns?'

'If the ship is as good as secure, seems to me a good idea to take them out and wrap the whole thing up,' I said. 'Go and tell Pete and the others I'm calling in Captain Wilson and the rest of our mob.'

'Got it,' nodded Marty, and he hurried back down below decks.

I went back to the bridge. Jerry and Mack were keeping watch over the bound and gagged crewmen.

'What's happening?' asked Mack. 'What's all that shooting about?'

'Some of the Marines decided to resist,' I said. 'All over now.'

'The prisoners?' asked Jerry.

'Marty says they're freeing them now,' I

replied. 'So, time to call up the Seventh Cavalry.'

I flicked on the radio-telephone in my helmet .

'Delta Four calling Delta One. Do you read? Over.'

There was a crackle in my headphones, then I heard Captain Wilson's voice say, 'Reading you. Over.'

'On board secure,' I reported. 'Ready for assault. Over.'

'Reading you. Over and out,' responded Wilson.

I turned to Mack.

'You OK to look after this lot on your own while me and Jerry do the honours outside?' I asked.

'Trussed up like they're chickens in a butcher's shop, what do you think?' demanded Mack indignantly.

Jerry and I returned to the deck and took up crouching positions by the handrail. From here we could see down on to the three machine-gun posts, partly hidden in the remains of the old whaling station. Each position had two men, one to fire the gun, one to keep it supplied with ammunition. The machine-guns were pointed inland. Jerry and I aimed our automatic rifles down at the machine-gun posts, and waited. We didn't have to wait long.

There was a burst of gunfire from the darkness inland as Captain Wilson's team opened up. Blinding red and white tracers poured into the enemy positions, some ricocheting off the bits of rusting machinery.

Immediately the Guantinian machine-gunners sprang into action, returning fire into the darkness, bullets spraying to the left and right in a wide fan. Then a flare went up, illuminating the harbour. That was our signal. Jerry and I opened fire, too, raining a fusillade of bullets down on to the shore around the machine-gun positions.

The machine-gunners quickly became aware that they were caught in crossfire, trapped by gunfire from both front and back. One of the gunners tried to turn his gun towards the ship. I let off a burst that smashed straight into his position.

'*Capitular o morir!*' I yelled. Surrender or die. It may have been a bit melodramatic, but it got the message across.

The response was immediate. The Guantinian machine-guns stopped firing. The soldiers manning them knelt down, facing towards me, putting their hands up as they did so.

Into my helmet microphone I said 'OK, Captain. We have the position secured.'

I caught a movement out of the corner of my eye and swung round, rifle raised in case one of the Guantinos on board was trying some last resistance. But it was just Pete who had come on to the deck, followed by the reason for our mission: the prisoners, now freed.

One of our Marines came over to me, a broad grin on his face, and slapped me heartily on the shoulder.

'Well done, you blokes!' he said happily. 'I always knew someone would come and rescue us. I might have known it would be the SAS!'

'Your own guys are with us,' I said. 'They'll be coming from our ship soon.'

Then I looked along the line of prisoners, and frowned. It didn't look to me like there were twenty men here. In fact, I counted just eight.

'Where are the others?' I asked.

Pete grimaced.

'Four are in the hospital bay. Along with these eight, that's all there are here. The rest were taken by the reinforcements who went to Solsborg. Looks like it ain't over yet, lads.'

Chapter 8
PLAN OF ACTION

Captain Wilson and most of his squad came aboard the *Paraiso*, bringing with them the six Guantinian soldiers from the machine-gun posts. Banco, Mick, Tony and Wiggy replaced them, keeping watch inland against any attack, although our guess was that there wouldn't be any Guantinian soldiers out there. They'd all be wrapped up twenty miles away at Solsborg.

I stayed on the bridge with Jake while he operated the radio, sending a message to the *Antrim* to let them know that the harbour and the ice-breaker were secured, and for them to join us. There were repeated radio calls from the Guantinians at Solsborg, but we ignored them. We hoped this would start them worrying about what was going on at Troon. The less they heard, the more their imagination would play tricks and make them think it was worse than it was. Perhaps a whole invasion forced had landed and taken the *Paraiso*, and were even now planning to attack them at Solsborg. We'd blown up their only helicopter, so they had no way of flying over us to find out what was really happening. They should really be panicking about now.

The great disappointment for me, and the rest of the lads, was that, although we'd managed to rescue eight of the Marines and four of the scientists, the other four Marines and four scientists were still in Guantinian hands. They had been on the convoy that had passed us on our way here. Again, they were being used as human shields. Our mission would not be over until these eight men were also released. Safely.

As Pete had reported, four of our Marines had been injured during the three days of fighting following the Guantinian invasion. They had bullet wounds, although one of them looked like some heavy armaments had hit him, because he'd lost both his legs. We were heartened to see that the *Paraiso*'s doctor had done a good job of looking after them. I knew the men themselves would feel a lot happier when they were transferred to our own medical facilities on the *Antrim*.

While we waited for the *Antrim* to arrive, it seemed an ideal opportunity for the whole squad to catch up on some much needed sleep. We all grabbed some shut-eye while Captain Wilson's men took over from us, guarding our Guantinian prisoners.

It seemed I'd hardly put my head down on the pillow in a bunk – a luxury after spending all that time out on the freezing cold island – when Jerry was shaking me awake.

'Rise and shine, Sleeping Beauty,' he said. 'The *Antrim*'s tied up alongside. We're about to get a briefing.'

'Where?' I asked.

'In the mess hall,' said Jerry. 'We eat while we listen. And real food for a change, not just rations.'

As we walked to the mess hall, we passed some of the Marines and the Commandos who were taking over the *Paraiso*, occupying the positions held by the Guantinians: radio operators, helm, deckhands, orderlies, and also jailers – only now it was the Guantinians who were under lock and key.

The mess hall was filling up as Jerry and I walked in. Most of the rest of our squad was there, plus the Marines and the scientists we'd rescued. Jerry and I helped ourselves to grub and then sat down at a table with Jake and Mack. Sitting next to them were some of the scientists. The first thing I noticed was that it didn't matter whether they were tall or short, fat or thin, or what colour their skin was, they all had one thing on common: big bushy beards and moustaches. I chucked to myself as I realized that, living out here in this frozen heap of rock where you needed as much protection from the weather as possible, one sure way of keeping your face warm was to grow a big beard and moustache.

'Jerry and Rob,' said Mack, doing the introductions as we sat down. 'This is Dr Eric Munro, leader of the British Antarctic Survey team,' he said, introducing the man sitting next to him.

'Good morning,' nodded Munro in greeting, adding a broad smile. 'As I've just said to your colleagues, we have to thank you for rescuing us like that. And with no loss of life. A quite remarkable achievement.'

'We do what we can,' said Jerry.

'All this must have come as a bit of a shock to you,' I said. 'Out here in the middle of nowhere, to suddenly find yourself in a war zone.'

'You can say that again,' commented the scientist next to Munro, an Australian. 'Frankly, when it all started we thought it was just a bit of a joke. I'm Joe Baker, by the way. Marine biologist.'

'Joe was the one who first saw the scrap-metal dealers raising the Guantinian flag after they landed,' explained Munro. 'Personally, knowing a bit of historical background about their claim to the island, I didn't think it so funny.'

'So Eric went along to Troon and offered to punch their lights out if they didn't take their flag down,' said Baker.

'Not at all,' corrected Munro. 'I asked them *very politely* to take their flag down. I also pointed out that, as the magistrate of the island, they had to apply to me first before any work was done.'

'And their reaction?' I asked.

Munro smiled uncomfortably.

'They laughed and said it was nothing to do with me. This island was their territory.'

'And that was when Eric offered to punch their lights out,' chuckled Baker.

Munro shrugged.

'I admit I lost my temper with them. But as there was just myself and Joe down at Troon, with about fifteen of these scrap-metal men –'

'All built like brick walls on legs,' put in Baker.

'I thought it best to pass the problem on to our governor on the main Lincoln Island. And the rest you know.'

'How did you get involved in the fighting?' asked Jerry.

'Reluctantly,' answered Munro. 'But we didn't really have much choice. The Guantinians launched a series of assaults. The Marines sent to defend the island retaliated. All we could do was stay at at Solsborg while the fighting went on around us. Luckily for us, the Guantinians decided not to use their really heavy weapons against our base.'

'Only because they knew they'd need the base afterwards, with winter coming on,' said Joe.

'Whatever the reason, they just fired rifles and machine-guns at the defensive positions our Marines had created round the base. The Marines fought really bravely, especially considering how heavily they were outnumbered. I'm surprised they were able to hold out against the attacks for so long.'

'So were we,' I said.

'To be honest, I think they'd have fought to the death,' said Baker. 'I think the only reason they finally surrendered was because they realized the only option the Guantinians had left was to use their heavy guns, and that could have wiped us out as well. They're a brave bunch of blokes.'

They certainly were, I thought. Twelve lightly armed Marines holding 200 heavily armed Guantinian Marines at bay for three days. That was courage under fire of the highest order.

A sharp knocking noise made us turn round. Captain Wilson was standing next to a map of South Carolina that he'd tacked to the wall.

'Good morning, gentlemen,' he began. 'To keep those of you who've been having forty winks up to date on the current situation: the four wounded British Marines have been taken on board the *Antrim*, as have two Guantinian soldiers injured in our successful assault to take the *Paraiso* and the harbour.

'There has been no attempt at contact from the Guantinians at Solsborg, or from their frigate, for the last five hours. In other words, they know something's happened here. We have to anticipate that they'll be taking precautions to protect themselves.

'I think it's unlikely that they'll send their frigate to try and attack us. The *Antrim* certainly hasn't picked it up on its radar. Plus, two of the *Antrim*'s Wessex helicopters flew sorties over Solsborg at dawn. They reported that the enemy appear to have decided to stay put.

'It looks as if we've got them pinned down. But I would remind you that there are a lot of them. Our freed prisoners have been giving us rough estimates of how many Guantinian Marines and soldiers were here. Our calculation is that there will be about one hundred and fifty enemy soldiers at Solsborg. We know they took heavy weapons with them. They also have their frigate for protection.

'Now, in normal circumstances it would be straightforward: we'd hit them with a heavy bombardment from the *Antrim*, then move in and mop up with a combined force of ourselves, the Marines and 42 Commando. But these are not normal circumstances. The Guantinians are still holding eight of our men prisoner at Solsborg. We can't start think about mounting a major attack until we get them out.'

Like me, all the SAS men nodded their heads. Normally our role was to get as close to the enemy positions as possible and mark the key targets: machine-gun posts, heavy artillery, ammunition stores, vehicles, and so on. If we were working with helicopter gunships, we'd mark them with a laser. The helicopters could home in on them and take them out. Or, if we were working with long-range armaments – like we were now with the *Antrim* on hand – we'd radio in the map coordinates of the target and they'd hit the target from where they where. That works only if the enemy isn't holding your own people prisoner. When armaments hit a target, they don't make any distinction between friend and foe.

As Captain Wilson said, we had to get the eight British Marines and scientists away from the base before the *Antrim* could open its attack on the Guantinian positions.

'So,' said Wilson, 'the plan is that we'll be leaving four of the SAS guys here at Troon, with the Marines, to guard the harbour and the *Paraiso*.' Turning towards Dr Munro he said: 'You and the rest of your team of scientists will also stay here, Dr Munro. 42 Commando will remain on board the *Antrim*. The *Antrim* will head out to sea and take up a position a few miles off Solsborg, and await our signal. The rest of D Squadron will head back to Solsborg overland to get our men out of the Guantinians' hands.'

'At least you'll have an easier journey,' said Dr Munroe. 'You can use the remaining ATV left here. That'll save you getting blisters on your feet!'

Jerry and I chuckled at this. Dr Munro looked surprised.

'Have I said something funny?' he asked.

'If only it were that simple,' said Captain Wilson. 'You see, after the Guantinians realized something was happening here, they probably erected road blocks or ambush points on the track to Solsborg. If we head back in the ATV, we might as well have a sign painted on it saying, "We're here. Please shoot us." No, I'm afraid that once again it's going to be the long march for us. Keeping off-track, staying away from anywhere they might have set up a position. Our aim is to get to Solsborg and release the rest of your colleagues, not to have a fire-fight before we get there.'

Dr Munro nodded.

'Excuse my ignorance,' he said. 'I know my colleagues will be safe now you're here. Who better than the SAS to mount a rescue mission, eh?'

As I ate my breakfast, I knew this would be my last hot food for a while. Another long march across freezing terrain faced us, and then a final confrontation with the massed Guantinian troops. The task ahead was daunting. We'd managed to rescue the first lot of prisoners by using an element of surprise. Getting to the remaining eight would be doubly difficult, because the Guantinians would be expecting us. They knew something had gone wrong for their men at Troon. Now they would be more on guard than ever. Plus the odds against us were overwhelming. At least 150 enemy soldiers. By now, too, the base must have been heavily fortified. Where would they be holding the prisoners? For all we knew, they could be on their frigate. And if that was the case, then we were in real trouble. Could we really free them?

Chapter 9
LAND-MINES

It was late morning when we set off. There were twelve of us in the squad heading for Solsborg. Nick, Tony, Wiggy and Dobbs had been left behind with the contingent of Marines to guard Troon harbour and the *Paraiso*.

Once again we were on skis and hauling the pulk loaded with our equipment behind us. Any doubts we had about the task ahead we put to the back of our minds. Everyone felt optimistic as we slid over the ice and snow. We had retaken the harbour at Troon. We had taken the huge ice-breaker. And we'd freed the twelve British prisoners being held on board without any loss of life, either to them or ourselves. That was something to be proud of. We had to remain positive about what lay ahead.

Having lost the ice-breaker, I was fairly sure the Guantinians wouldn't let the frigate be an easy target. The *Paraiso*'s civilian crew weren't as well trained as their military equivalents and weren't as tight about security. Getting on board the *Paraiso* had been relatively easy. Getting on board a Guantinian frigate without being noticed would be a different matter entirely.

As before, the terrain was difficult going. When the snow was replaced by frozen scrubland and rocks, we took off the skis and marched. We put the skis back on when we hit another stretch of snow. It made for frustratingly slow progress.

As we had done on our journey to Troon, we kept two miles inland from the track, but parallel to it. We were still clothed in our all-white Arctic camouflage outfits, ready to drop to the ground at a second's notice if we heard or saw any movement. The track appeared to be clear of the enemy. I wondered where they would be waiting for us. Where would the ambush be? They would know for sure that we'd be returning to Solsborg for the remaining prisoners. Somewhere between Troon and the Solsborg they would have set a trap. I could feel my heart pounding as I thought about it and did my best to get myself under control. Having your senses on full alert is vital; having them out of control is dangerous.

After two hours we'd only covered seven miles. Thirteen to go, and still no sign of the enemy. We paused while the men switched pulk-hauling duties, with Zed and Marty taking over from Banco and Mick. I turned and saw Jerry studying the track through his binoculars. He seemed to be looking at something very intently.

'What have you seen?' I asked.

'I'm not sure,' he said. 'Take a look at the track. Tell me what you see there.'

I put my binoculars to my eyes.

'Bits of ice,' I said. 'Small rocks. Snow. Tracks of the trucks and ATVs from where they went along it.'

'Anything else?'

I peered harder. There was something in the snow. Markings of some sort.

'Footprints?'

'Why would the Guantinians get out of their vehicles in the middle of nowhere?' asked Jerry.

'To set an ambush,' I suggested.

'In that case, where is it?' asked Jerry.

The answer struck us both at the same time.

'Mines!' we said together.

Captain Wilson and the rest of the squad had turned to see what we were up to. I gestured them over to our position.

'What have you got?' asked Wilson.

'Jerry and I are fairly sure they've mined the track,' I told him.

Wilson put his binoculars to his eyes and looked at where I was pointing.

'Possible,' he said.

'Only one way to find out,' said Jerry.

Wilson nodded.

'OK,' he said. 'You found 'em, your unit checks 'em.'

'Great,' groaned Jake. 'Well done, you two. Now we're on land-mine-clearing detail.'

The rest of the squad took up positions in outcrops of rock behind us, ready to give us covering fire if needed. Me, Jake, Jerry and Mack took off our skis and headed for the track in crouching runs, zigzagging all the time. We kept our heads down as low as we could, keeping watch all the time in case there was an ambush waiting for us.

Luckily for us, the snow was thin here, just a shallow crust that crunched under our boots as we moved. We made it to the track. No one shot at us.

I looked at the footprints on the track. Near them there were small mounds where the snow had been piled up. No wind had done that. They had been made by hand.

'Back off,' I told the others. 'No sense in us all being blown to bits if I get it wrong.'

'I saw them first,' said Jerry. 'I'm staying with you.'

Mack and Jake were about to argue that they too would stay and check the mounds with us, but then they saw sense. If anything did go wrong and Jerry and I were killed or injured, that would mean two less in our squad. We couldn't afford another two as well. Jake and Mack moved back about fifty metres away from the edge of the track.

I put my rifle down and slowly moved forwards on my hands and knees to the mound nearest me. Very gently I pushed my finger into the base of the mound. Nothing. No metal. Slowly, very slowly, I started to clear the packed snow. I was counting on the mine being the type with the trigger at the top which is why I was working my way in from the side. If I was wrong and the trigger mechanism was at the side, and I accidentally knocked against it ... At worst, it would blow me to bits; at best, I'd lose my arm and most of my face.

Gently, very gently, I cleared round the raised centre of the mound, pulling off lumps of caked and frozen snow and ice. Then there it was ... the dull sheen of metal glinting in the chilly daylight. I cleared more snow and exposed the trigger fully: a flat, round, metal disc. Just waiting to be pushed down to set off the explosives beneath.

I looked at Jerry and he nodded in agreement: we'd confirmed our suspicions.

'Got it,' I said into the microphone of my helmet. 'Definitely a land-mine.'

'How many of them?' asked Captain Wilson in my headphones.

I looked along the track. There were another three mounds in each direction, each marked by frozen footprints around them.

'Seven over a distance of about fifteen metres,' I replied. 'Frankly, Captain, I can't see it's worth our while defusing them. There could be loads more scattered all the way on the track. Add up the time it would take us to find each one and then disarm it, it's a job that will take days.'

There was a pause, then Captain Wilson said, 'Agreed. We'll radio our boys at Troon and on the *Antrim* and warn them to stay off the track until they get word it's clear. We'll move on.'

Now, confident that the land-mines were our only danger, me, Jerry, Jake and Mack hurried back to join the rest of the squad. Frog was already sending a coded message on the radio to the *Antrim* for them to pass on to our boys at Troon, warning them about the mines.

Then we set off again. One danger had been avoided. What lay ahead?

Chapter 10

BACK AT SOLSBORG

It was late afternoon by the time we arrived within telescope range of Solsborg. Daylight was already starting to fade. When you're this far south, there's more night than there is day in winter. Working on the principle that if we could see them, they could see us, four of us – me, Jerry, Jake and Mack – crawled forwards to take observation. The rest of the squad stayed hidden behind a cluster of rocks.

We worked our way forwards on our elbows and knees until we came to a low ridge that we could use for cover. The BAS base at Solsborg was no longer just a small group of four huts. Even from this distance, and in the gloom of gathering dusk, I could see that it had been turned into an armed camp. Machine-gun posts were stationed all round it.

It looked like a small town of tents had sprung up around the huts. I counted thirty tents. Four men to a tent meant 120 Guantinians. Plus the men stationed in the huts – estimated at nearly fifty on our previous visit. We were facing about 170 enemy Marines – more than we had anticipated back at Troon.

A perimeter fence of coils of barbed wire stretched round the camp. It was supported at intervals by cairns of rocks. Along this boundary, soldiers were trying to hammer fence posts into the frozen ground. Rolls of wire were piled up near by, waiting to be attached to the posts. The soldiers weren't having much luck. As they dug they either struck rock, or their pickaxes and shovels just bounced off the icy ground.

Overshadowing the whole encampment was the frigate tied up in the small harbour. Some people hear the word 'frigate' and think of a small ship. In fact many frigates are as big as a modern destroyer. This one must have been about 150 metres long, with a beam (width) of fifteen metres. I recognized it from my time in the Marines as one of the Broadsword class. It had a powerful array of weapons: eight Harpoon anti-ship missiles, two SAM launchers with thirty-two missiles, as well as a 4.5in gun. In addition, it bristled with heavy machine and anti-aircraft guns. Beneath the water line I knew it had two triple tubes for firing torpedoes. Usually it also carried a helicopter, but since we'd blown it to bits, that particular piece of armament had gone.

The reason I knew so much about the frigate was because it was a British ship. The Guantinians had bought it, like most of their fleet, from Britain. That's the trouble with selling weapons to an ally: one day that ally may turn into your enemy.

A frigate of this size normally has a crew of 250. Add that figure to the 170 Marines, and we were facing odds of over 400 against our twelve.

'We're going to need a diversion,' muttered Jake. 'Getting on board the ice-breaker from the sea was a crafty move, but they won't be caught by that trick again.'

'And even if we did take the ship first, they still outnumber us big-time on land,' added Mack.

'Agreed,' nodded Captain Wilson.

'Maybe the *Antrim* could launch a few missiles?' suggested Marty.

'Not a good idea,' said Pete. 'If we get a fire-fight between the two ships, there's no knowing which one would come off worse.'

It was a good point. The *Antrim* and the Guantinian frigate were pretty evenly matched for size and gun-strength. The *Antrim* was a little longer and a little wider than the Guantinian frigate, but not by much. When it came to firepower, the *Antrim* had two 4.5in guns, two 40mm and two 20mm guns, one large gun more than the Guantinian frigate. However we all knew it had one major disadvantage.

'The *Antrim* can't fire at the frigate or the camp for fear of hitting the prisoners,' Captain Wilson said. 'And the Guantinians know that.'

Banco gestured towards the four ATVs parked up. Two were at the east side of the camp, two at the west.

'How about blowing one of them up?' he suggested. 'We could hit it with a missile. While they're chasing in one direction, two blokes go in from the other side and find the prisoners.'

'From what we've seen of this lot, they're more likely to head in the other direction, away from the blast,' I commented.

'Rob's right,' said Jerry. 'Plus an attack like that would put them on edge. They've already lost their position at Troon.'

'So, what do you suggest?' asked Captain Wilson.

Jerry thought about it for a second, then he said: 'Something to make them relax a bit.'

'A false message,' said Mack. 'Something they pick up on their radios that says we're not going to do anything.'

'Right,' nodded Jerry. 'You can bet they'll be listening to all radio traffic, trying to intercept messages between us and the *Antrim*, or between us and the boys at Troon.'

'An excellent idea,' said Captain Wilson. 'Jerry, send a coded message to Troon. Tell them we're going to send them a message in about twenty minutes. But instead of transmitting in code, we're going to make a deliberate mistake. We're going to send a message to them saying, "Confirm withdraw all personnel away from Solsborg back to Troon with immediate effect." The commander at Troon is to get annoyed and transmit a telling-off in reply saying something like: "You're on an open channel. Do you want to give our strategy away to the enemy, you idiots!" Then we go to radio silence.

'They're bound to have an English-speaking communications officer listening in, just as we've got Spanish speakers on the *Antrim* trying to pick up any of their communications.

'With luck, they'll think they're safe and their guard will be down. My guess is, once they get that message, they'll stop work on that boundary fence. For one thing, in about thirty minutes it's going to be too dark for them to work. OK, they could work by artificial light, but as we all know, winter nights in the Arctic aren't the best conditions.'

Captain Wilson was right. If it's cold during daylight hours in the Arctic, during night-time everything really freezes. And it's hard swinging a pickaxe or wielding a shovel when you're wrapped up from head to foot like a polar bear.

'Who are the Spanish speakers?' asked Captain Wilson.

'Me, Captain,' I said.

'And me,' put in Zed.

'*Buenas noches*,' added Frog with a grin. '*A donde va usted?*'

'*Tiene algo mejor?*' I responded, also with a grin.

'All right, you three,' said Wilson. 'You're the chosen ones. Once we've sent the fake message and night falls, in you go.'

Chapter 11
INTO THE CAMP

Night fell, and with it the temperature. If it had been cold before, now it was seriously sub-zero. And with the night came rain. Not normal rain, but a terrible drizzle of thin slivers of ice which froze to your skin as the wind blew them on to you. Luckily, our camouflage gear protected us from the worst of this. Nothing but our eyes were showing, forcing us to squint to try and stop the icy drizzle from getting into them.

On a snowy landscape at night any movement sticks out like a sore thumb, especially if you're on the look-out for it. However, tonight there was a cloudy sky. No moon, no stars, no twilight. Visibility was poor. Exactly what we'd been hoping for.

'Go,' came Captain Wilson's voice through the headset in my helmet.

We moved from our forward position one

at a time. First me, crouching low, then dropping down to lie flat, my rifle aimed towards the base. Then Frog past after me, also crouching, rifle cocked and ready, then dropping flat after a few metres and taking up forward guard, point position. I turned to face the rear as Zed moved up, overtaking both me and Frog, moving our point position a few metres further forwards before dropping flat. As Frog turned to face the rear, I moved forwards again. And so we continued, slowly advancing on the base.

Leap-frogging our positions like this, we eventually reached the roll of barbed wire that formed the perimeter fence. We got there without being spotted by any of the machine-gun posts. My guess was that the poor blokes manning them were huddled up against the freezing cold, reassured that no one would be attacking them because of the fake 'radio message' they'd intercepted.

I pulled out my wire cutters and gestured for Frog and Zed to each hold the wire firmly in their gloved hands either side of where I was going to cut it. I mimed holding the wire with one hand and making a cutting motion with my fingers. You get good at making yourself understood without words when you're on a mission. Out in the field, it's all hand signals.

Zed and Frog grabbed the wire firmly. I pressed the handles of my cutters and the wire parted. The other two carefully rolled their end away to the nearest cairn, where they used stones to hold it firmly in place. We now had our way in, and our way out.

To get from the perimeter to the tents, there was no question of us crouching and running. From here it was crawling on our bellies, snake-style, without making any noise. Which is difficult to do when you're also holding an automatic rifle. The only way to do it is very slowly, slithering a bit at a time. It helped that the ground had been trampled down during the day by soldiers trying to put up the fence posts. Their boots had turned the snow into slush, that had now become a sheet of ice.

The three of us slid and slithered over this ice, heading for the nearest tent.

All the time I kept glancing behind me towards the machine-gun posts. But all I could see in the gloom were the men's backs. Luckily for us, no one was turning round to look in towards the camp.

As we reached the nearest tent, we got to our feet in a crouch. We were no longer exposed. The tents gave us cover. I located the toilet block, remembering where it was from my last visit here. I was counting on one of the 170 men in the camp needing to go to the toilet at some point in the night.

Me, Zed and Frog reached the toilet block. You couldn't mistake it. Even with these freezing low temperatures, the smell gave it away.

We crept inside.

It was empty. In addition to the urinals and the showers, there were three toilet cubicles. Zed went into one, shutting the door. Frog and I went into another. That meant that anyone coming in to use the toilet only had one choice of cubicle.

We waited in silence. A minute passed. Then two minutes. Then three. We remained deadly still, waiting patiently. The ability to wait is a vital skill that we're trained for in the SAS, and we certainly get lots of opportunity to use it. In ditches. In huts. Watching a pool in a jungle. Sometimes for days on end. Only in this situation we didn't have days. We didn't have hours, either. We had to get this sorted out quickly.

Five minutes passed, and there was still no sign of anyone. I was just thinking that if no one came we'd have to slip into one of the tents and grab someone, when I heard the noise of the door of the toilet block being opened. Immediately, Zed and I readied ourselves. We heard the sound of boots on concrete, then the door of the only available cubicle open and shut.

Before the man could shoot the bolt to lock the door of the cubicle, I leapt out and kicked the door inwards, hard.

The door smacked the Guantinian in the back, propelling him forwards. He stumbled and fell towards the toilet bowl, stopping himself just in time. Before he could yell out, I was on him, my hand firmly over his mouth.

In Spanish I whispered: 'If you struggle or try to make a noise, I will kill you. Do you understand?'

I turned the soldier round to face me, keeping my hand over his mouth all the while. At the sight of my face pressed close to his, but wearing a black balaclava which only showed my eyes, and Zed standing beside me – similarly clothed but pointing an automatic rifle straight at him – the soldier's eyes bulged with fear.

'Do you understand?' I repeated.

The soldier nodded, jerking his head up and down nervously.

'I am about to take my hand away from your mouth,' I said in Spanish. 'If you make a sound until I tell you to, my friend here will blow your head off. You will die, and as soon as the shooting starts, all your comrades here will die. We are not here to kill you. We only want information. Do you understand?'

Again the soldier nodded. Even though it was freezing cold, the sweat of fear was thick on his forehead.

'*Bueno*,' I said.

I took my hand away from his mouth and stepped back a pace. Zed kept the barrel of his rifle firmly fixed on the soldier's face, right between his eyes.

'Where are the British prisoners?' I asked.

The Guantinian was going to try and lie. I could tell by his eyes, the sudden rapid movement from side to side, a combination of fear and self-survival. He was young, about eighteen. Only a year younger than me, but with so much less experience of warfare. I felt that decades rather than months separated us. As he opened his mouth to speak, I put my finger to his lips.

'You are about to lie to me,' I said quietly. 'You are about to say that they are not here. That would annoy me very much. I know they are in this place. Four British soldiers and four scientists. Now, where are they?'

I didn't need to raise my voice or get angry. He could tell by my eyes that I would know if he tried to lie to me, and he knew that if he did I would hurt him very badly.

I could see his mind working, asking himself questions: what will happen if I tell this man where they are? Perhaps they will still kill me? What will my commanding officer say?

Then he saw Frog come into his line of vision, also holding his rifle.

'He doesn't know,' said Frog in Spanish. 'Let's kill him and find someone else who does.'

That did it. The fear kicked in. It didn't

occur to the Guantinian to ask himself why, if Frog meant it, Frog had spoken in Spanish and not in English.

'They are in the big hut,' he burst out, his voice a hoarse whisper.

I felt a sense of relief. I had dreaded him telling us they were being held on the frigate. Trying to get them off it without major loss of life would have been almost impossible.

I remembered the description of the base that we'd read about in our briefing papers on our journey on the *Antrim*. Four huts. Two for accommodation. One for toilets and showers. And the big hut, the operations centre, which also housed the stores at one end in a large wire cage.

That made sense. With the perimeter fence not yet ready, if the prisoners had been kept in a tent, or in an ordinary hut, they had a chance of escaping. But locked in a wire cage was as good as any prison cell. With the added bonus that they were at the centre of activities and communications, permanently visible. Any attack we made on the big hut would run the risk of hitting our own men inside it.

'OK,' I said to the others. 'Looks like

some breaking and entering is called for.'
Turning back to our prisoner, I asked him
in Spanish how many Guantinian soldiers
were in the big hut.

'*No se,*' he said. I don't know.

In Spanish, Frog told him in low
menacing tones that it might be a good
idea if he tried to hazard a guess, if he
wanted to remain healthy.

Hastily, our prisoner began guessing:
'*Seis, siete, ocho ...*' Six, seven, eight.

'Not bad odds,' commented Zed.

'Providing he's right,' I said. 'My guess is
he's so scared of what Frog is going to do
to him if he stays quiet that he's just
saying the first things that come into his
head. There could be twenty of them in
there.'

'Only one way to find out ...' said Frog.

Zed and I nodded. It was time for the
moment of truth.

We were going in.

Chapter 12

UNDER FIRE

I turned to our prisoner.

'*Gracias*,' I said. 'We are going to take you with us to the big hut, but I give you my word, as long as you do not raise the alarm, you will be safe. If you try and raise the alarm by any way at all, I will kill you. I do not need a gun to do it.' I pulled out my knife and held it up so that he could see the blade. 'You will be dead and no one will be any the wiser. Do you understand?'

Again, the Guantinian nodded.

Holding the point of my knife against his back so that he could feel it, I pushed him forwards out of the toilet block. Zed and Frog followed, their rifles cradled in their arms, ready to use if necessary. I had looped my rifle over my shoulder.

We moved out of the dim light that glowed from the windows of the toilet block towards the big hut, as our prisoner had called it. We made it to the door of the hut without meeting anyone else. I put my ear to the door and listened. There were voices talking in Spanish, a bit of laughter, then more talking. It was too muffled for me to hear exactly what they were discussing.

Zed and Frog looked at me quizzically. I nodded and gave them a thumbs up. I stepped back from the door, holding our prisoner with one hand, while Zed stepped up to the door. He turned the door handle gently, and then slammed the door open hard and rushed in, crouching low, his rifle held steady.

I went in next, with the prisoner in front of me, and Frog bringing up the rear. As I pushed the prisoner away from me, I brought up my rifle and swept it around the room. I was aware as I did it that it was important that we did this without any shooting if possible. The last thing we wanted was to wake the rest of the camp and have them joining in.

Within a second I took in the scene. There were six soldiers in the hut: one wearing headphones at the radio set, three others sitting on chairs by a burning stove, and two others standing. They turned as we had rushed in and now they gaped at us, stunned. Out of the corner of my eye I saw the cage at the end of the room, and was aware of men behind the wire.

Suddenly one of the enemy soldiers, an officer, snapped out of his initial shock and moved, his hand reaching down to the holster on his hip, going for his pistol.

BANG!

It wasn't the crack of a bullet, but it might as well have been from the effect it had on everyone. Frog had pulled out a grenade and thrown it, with the pin still in, hard and fast, straight at the Guantinian officer. It had hit him smack between the eyes with a crunch of metal against flesh and bone that made your head ache just to hear it.

The officer crumpled as if he'd been kicked in the head by a horse and fell to the floor in a heap.

Frog winked at me.

'I knew all those years playing darts would come in useful one day,' he said. 'Double top, eight times out of ten.'

I waved the barrel of my rifle at the other soldiers, who had all put their hands up as soon as the officer had hit the floor. Having seen what Frog could do with an unarmed grenade, they were obviously well aware that with a live one, or even a gun, he was probably really deadly.

'The keys,' I snapped in Spanish, gesturing at the wire cage. 'Open the door. Now.'

Frog and Zed kept the rest of the soldiers covered while I went with the soldier who had the keys to the cage. The eight men behind the wire watched as the soldier fumbled putting the key into the padlock that held the cage door shut. It was fairly easy to distinguish between the scientists – who looked shocked – and the Marines, who were obviously delighted by our arrival. A quick assessment told me no one was seriously hurt, although one of the Marines had bruises down one side of his face and a healing gash above his left eye.

As the door swung open, they tumbled out.

'No noise,' I told them. 'We're getting out of here quietly, if we can.'

The Marine with the bruised face looked down at the officer lying unconscious on the floor.

'That's who gave me these,' he said, pointing at his bruises. 'I'm glad you gave him something back.'

'Where are Dr Munro and the others?' asked one of the scientists.

'They're all safe,' I said. 'We've taken Troon and the ice-breaker they were being held on.'

'Good,' said a Marine. 'I guessed something was up when the radio link went dead. It threw the Guantinians into a right panic while they tried to work out what had happened. We hopped you'd be along here next.'

'Until we heard the message about pulling back from Solsborg,' added another. 'That pulled the rug from under us, I can tell you.'

'It was a fake,' said Zed. 'Aimed at lulling the enemy into a false sense of security.'

'Can I suggest we do all the talking when we're out of here,' cut in Frog.

'Good idea,' said a scientist.

'First, it might be a good idea to tie and gag these guys,' I said, indicating the enemy soldiers. They were all still standing with their hands up, wondering what we were going to do next. 'Any rope in those stores?'

'Loads of it,' said one of the Marines. 'It'll be a pleasure to give a hand tying up these characters .'

'I'll disable the radio,' said Frog. 'No sense in leaving them with a way to contact that ship out there, if they do get free.'

I grinned as Frog set about taking parts of the radio out to leave it useless, and Zed and the Marines started tying up the enemy soldiers. Zed was an expert on knots, as would the Marines be. I doubted if any of the enemy would be able to break free after Zed and the Marines had finished with them.

I kept apart from the action, pointing my rifle at the soldiers as a reminder not try anything.

'Right,' said Zed as he tied up the last soldier. 'That's us finished here. How's the radio, Frog?'

'Out of action.'

'Good.' Turning to the eight prisoners we'd freed, I told them: 'We've got an escape route all ready made – a hole in the perimeter wire. These two guys will go first, you eight follow them. I'll bring up the rear. OK?'

They nodded.

'OK,' they said.

'Right,' I said. 'Let's go.'

We left the big hut, Zed and Frog in the lead, the eight men following in single file, and me bringing up the tail end. I walked backwards, crab-like, rifle barrel sweeping from side to side, keeping low, eyes and ears alert for any sight or sound in the camp.

Zed and Frog moved the pace on, moving from shadow to shadow, from the big hut to the toilet block, then to the nearest tent, then to a tent nearer the perimeter, and so on. Every now and then they stopped to listen, and the eight freed men stopped as well. I kept my attention on the machine-gun posts. Still quiet.

Finally we made it to the perimeter of the camp, to the stretch of barbed wire that we'd cut. The nearest cover was a low ridge about fifty metres away. It had been one thing for three of us to cover that ground, crawling all the way, but getting eleven of us across that exposed patch of land without being spotted was going to be a real challenge.

'Crawl or run?' whispered Zed.

'Crawl,' I whispered back. 'Two at a time. Frog goes first with one of the scientists, to show the way. Then two at a time after that at three-second intervals. You and me stay at the back and go last. If things go wrong, then we start running.'

Zed nodded.

'OK,' he said. 'Off you go, Frog. When you get there, call in the others, just in case.'

Frog lowered himself flat and pulled one of the scientists down to the ground with him.

'Keep as flat as you can. Use your knees and elbows to push yourself along. Stay with me.'

The scientist nodded, obviously terrified but willing to do anything to get out there. He and Frog set off over the icy ground. I counted one ... two ... three, then Zed signalled for the next two to follow them. Another three seconds, then another two set off, crawling as fast as they could towards the darkness and the low ridge. Then another two. Then another pair.

Just me and Zed and one of the Marines were left, ready to go, when suddenly there came a splash from the darkness. It was only a small splash as one of the men slipped and fell through a thin crust of ice into a bog, but it was enough. It sounded like a explosion because the camp was so silent.

The machine-gunner nearest to us suddenly jerked into action, turning his gun towards the sound and firing blindly, sending tracers of bullets into the sky at head height. It was lucky the men had been crawling, or one or more of them would have been killed for certain.

'OK,' I said to Zed. 'Looks like you start running. Get going as soon as I hold them down.'

I aimed my rifle at the machine-gun post and let off a burst of automatic fire. There were screams and the machine-gun stopped firing. Then it started again, and I saw it swing around towards me.

'Go!' I yelled.

Zed was already moving, running and firing at the same time, and urging the last Marine forwards.

'Keep your head down!' he yelled. 'Zigzag!'

The other machine-gun posts now also sprung into life, the sound of its guns tearing through the night. As I ran for the low ridge, close behind Zed, I stopped and turned and fired round after round at it, before running again.

Now there was gunfire coming from our men. Captain Wilson and the rest of our squad had come up behind the ridge and were giving us covering fire. The noise of machine-gun fire coming at me from both directions was deafening.

I paused to fire one last burst at the nearest machine-gun post. Suddenly I felt a smack on my thigh and a pain that seemed to tear my body in half. I felt myself being thrown up into the air and then crashing down on to the ground.

Chapter 13
WOUNDED

As I lay there on the frozen ground I felt blood pouring out of my thigh. I tried to get up, but couldn't. My thigh bone was smashed. I heard a fusillade of shots and felt bits of ice and rock smash up into my face as enemy machine-gun bullets burst around me. I tried to turn to aim my rifle back at the camp. Then there was a burst of machine-gunfire and a savage pain went right through me as a bullet hit my left arm, tearing my rifle out of my grasp. My left hand dangled useless and broken at the end of my arm. Frantically, I tried to reach for my rifle with my right hand, but again the machine-gun opened up on me.

BOOOM!!!

The machine-gun fire stopped abruptly as a grenade exploded. I could hear the screams of the men at the post and smell the burning of cloth and cordite.

Then I felt hands gripping me under the armpits.

'We've got you, Rob,' said Zed's voice. 'We're getting you out of here.'

As I began to drift in and out of consciousness, I felt myself being lifted and half dragged, half carried, while all around me the sound of gunfire carried on.

What happened after that isn't really clear. All my concentration went into trying to deal with the screaming pain in my leg and my arm. When you get shot there is usually a feeling of numbness after the initial pain as the body tries to cope. But that soon wears off and then there's just pain. As the guys hauled me to safety behind the ridge, my whole body screamed out with every jarring movement. I forced my good hand into my mouth and bit down on it to stop myself from yelling out loud with agony.

There's no time for niceties when you're under fire. I felt myself dumped down, and then someone set to work on my leg. I think it was Zed, but I couldn't be sure. I could feel movement and realized that he was strapping my leg to my rifle, using it as a temporary splint. There were voices, instructions being issued, barked out above me, the *rat-a-tat-tat*, *rat-a-tat-tat* sound of gunfire, but all I could feel was pain.

'Blood,' I whispered. I knew I was losing blood from both my arm and my leg and I was afraid I was going to die because of it.

'Under control, mate,' said a voice. Jerry. So Jerry was here as well.

I felt myself being pulled about, lifted and rolled, and then dumped back on the ground again, but my sight was going, I couldn't see ... There was a mist over my eyes. I heard the sound of an enormous explosion that seemed to lift me up from the ground ... And then nothing ...

Chapter 14
HOMEWARD BOUND

I woke.

There was noise. Clattering. Voices. But not shouting. Nor shooting. The sound of boots on metal.

I opened my eyes.

Tubes. I was connected by tubes to something. I tried to turn my head to see what it was. A drip. I was attached to a drip. Two drips.

'He's awake.'

Jake's voice.

'About time. I was starting to get hungry.'

Mack's voice.

I forced myself to look at them, trying to focus, but their faces remained blurred.

'Hi,' I said. The voice didn't sound like mine; it sounded like it was coming through a tunnel of cotton wool.

'He's semi-conscious, so now perhaps you'd leave and come back when he's fully conscious.'

Another voice. An unfamiliar one, belonging to someone in a white coat.

'OK,' I heard Jerry say. 'But take good care of him. He's our mate.'

And then I felt as if I was falling down into a hole and just drifting ... drifting ...

I remember waking up again, hearing voices, and then drifting back to sleep. It all seemed a jumble. I began to think that I was back in England, but that didn't make sense. Who were all these people in white? And what was that noise? A sort of humming noise.

'It's the ship's engines,' said a voice. Jerry's voice.

I opened my eyes fully. The fuzziness had gone.

'Ship's engines?' I repeated, feeling stupid.

Jerry was sitting by my bed.

'We're on the *Antrim*,' he said. 'You're going to be OK.'

'What happened?' I asked.

'You took a bullet in your thigh that

broke the thigh bone, and one in the arm. You're going to be out of action for a bit.'

'I remember that,' I said. 'I mean, what happened afterwards? I heard more gunfire and then explosions ...'

'That was the *Antrim* firing,' said Jerry. 'Once we'd got the prisoners out and beyond the perimeter, Captain Wilson radioed the *Antrim* that the camp and the frigate were clear. Wham! The *Antrim* didn't hesitate. They wanted to take advantage of the confusion and chaos you, Frog and Zed had created when freeing the prisoners. So they started their bombardment before the Guantinians had time to sort themselves out.

'You should have seen it. Those big guns really have an impact. First they hit the Guantinian frigate, and then they started on the camp.'

'We were lucky they didn't hit us,' I commented. 'How are the rest of the guys? Anyone else injured?'

Jerry shook his head.

'No, we were lucky. You were our only casualty. Some of the enemy were hit when the *Antrim* started its heavy shelling. But they didn't have to keep it up for long. The

Guantinians surrendered almost at once. The machine-guns stopped firing and the men came out and started waving these white sheets. That was it. All over.'

'And now?'

'The Commandos and Marines are mopping up, sorting out the prisoners. Getting the mines lifted from the track. The rest of the task force are well on their way south. Aircraft carrier. Destroyers. The lot. There's no way the Guantinians are going to want to tangle with all that. Once they get here, you're going to be transferred to a fully equipped hospital ship with every care and attention. They'll soon have you up and about and back in action.'

I gave him a grin.

'We did it, though,' I said. 'Against overwhelming odds. We took our island back.'

'Of course we did. That's what we do,' said Jerry. 'We're the SAS.'

HISTORICAL NOTE

Although this book is fiction, it is based on events that actually happened. On Friday 19 March 1982 a party of Argentinian scrap dealers landed at the derelict whaling station at Leith, on South Georgia Island in the South Atlantic, and raised the Argentinian flag. When the British Antarctic Survey team on the island discovered this, they reported the incident to Governor Rex Hunt in Port Stanley, the capital of the Falkland Islands, 900 miles away. (South Georgia was part of the Falklands.) Hunt gave orders to the leader of the scientists – who also held the post of Magistrate of South Georgia – that the Argentinians must obtain authorization from him to work on the island. The Argentinians refused to do so.

The Falklands had been under British sovereignty since 1833, but Argentina had long-standing claims over the islands. The Argentinian Government ordered the ice-breaker *Bahia Paraiso*, with a large contingent of Marines on board, to sail to South Georgia to protect the scrap dealers. At the same time, a small party of British Marines were sent there from the Falkland Islands.

On 25 March, the Argentinian Marines landed on South Georgia. On 2 April, Argentinian forces invaded the main group of Falkland Islands. The conflict between Britain and Argentina now turned into a full-scale war. A task force was assembled in Britain and sent to the South Atlantic to recover the Falkland Islands.

After a series of battles, the British Marines on South Georgia were forced to surrender to overwhelming Argentinian forces.

The first step by the British task force was the retaking of South Georgia, code-named Operation Paraquat. A party of men from SAS D Squadron landed there from three helicopters in appalling conditions on 21 April. With the aid of a bombardment from their offshore support ship, the HMS *Antrim*, they launched attacks on the Argentinian positions and on the two harbours of Leith and Grytviken. They forced the Argentinians to surrender on 26 April.

The battle for the rest of the Falkland Islands was to continue for much longer.

MAP: THE FALKLAND ISLANDS

MAP: SOUTH GEORGIA

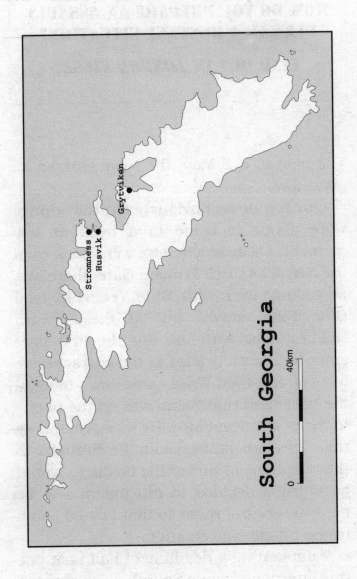

The next day, 5 May, the siege entered its sixth day.

Our top brass obviously felt that things were about to come to a head at any moment, because when we went back from the barracks to 15 Prince's Gate, there was no change-over with Blue Team. Instead Blue Team stayed put at the Forward Holding Area with us. For the first time since we'd been briefed at the barracks, we were all together. Word came down to us in the basement that Salim was on the phone to the police negotiator. He was demanding that an Arab ambassador be brought to the telephone or one of the hostages would be killed. I decided to nip upstairs to be near the control room so that I could listen to the phone conversation.

'I am setting a deadline of half past one this afternoon,' came Salim's voice over the

146

speaker connected to the phone. I recognized his voice because I'd heard it before on the speaker and on TV.

'Be reasonable, Salim,' the negotiator said, his voice calm, doing his best to appeal to the terrorist. 'It's impossible to get hold of an Arab ambassador so quickly. But the good news is that the imam at the Regent's Park mosque has offered to come in and mediate. I'm sure you can trust him.'

'That's not enough!' snapped Salim. 'You are not listening to me.'

'I am listening, Salim –' began the negotiator.

But Salim interrupted him and shouted angrily, 'I will kill a hostage unless an Arab ambassador is on this phone by half past one this afternoon.'

Then the speaker went dead.

I hurried downstairs and told the others what I'd heard.

'It's a bluff,' said Terry. 'We've had deadline after deadline, but has he killed any of the hostages yet?'

'This one could be different,' I said. 'Salim sounded really strung up.'

'Trust me, it's another bluff,' insisted

Terry. 'Think about what's happened so far. What's he done to the hostages? He's let them go, one by one. Four of them so far.' He shook his head. 'He's not going to start shooting them now. Not after six days.' He yawned. 'If you ask me, we're wasting our time here. Still, it gives us a chance to watch the snooker championship in comfort.'

Personally, I didn't share Terry's view of the situation. I had heard Salim's voice: it was a voice of a man under stress. And then there was the evidence from Mr Tarkuff. He had impressed me as a man who watched and worked things out. A man who knew where trouble would be coming from. It was the sort of second sense you get when you're a soldier, or a journalist working in war zones. Mr Tarkuff had spent five days in close proximity to the terrorists and if he thought things were going to go bad, things *were* going to be bad. I reckoned we had to be prepared.

I mentioned my opinion to Chris, and he nodded in agreement.

'Let's go up to the control room,' he said. 'See what we can find out.'

*

As the clock ticked away towards the deadline of 13.30, Chris and I went upstairs to the phone to the terrorists. We stayed out of the way, not wanting to get ordered back to the basement. As we stood there, the phone rang. The police negotiator picked it up. Then we heard the voice of PC Jimmy Preston over the speaker.

'PC Preston here. I have to warn you that one of the hostages has been tied to the banisters downstairs. They are threatening to shoot him if an Arab ambassador does not come to this phone at once.'

'I'm sorry,' said the negotiator. 'There hasn't been enough time for us to get an ambassador here, but –'

He was interrupted by a voice shouting angrily, 'You are lying!'

It was Salim, beside himself with rage. Either that, or, as Mr Tarkuff had said, he was under pressure to prove to the other terrorists that he could get them out of this, and he thought that shouting at the police would help him.

'Salim, believe me, I am not lying –' began the negotiator in a gentle and concerned tone of voice, but Salim cut him off again.

'The deadline has passed!' he yelled. 'I warned you what would happen if it passed and an ambassador did not speak to us. Let this be a lesson to you! This one is the first to die!'

The room was filled with the sound of a machine-gun being fired, followed by a scream. Then the speaker went dead.

Read more in Puffin

For complete information about books available from Puffin – and Penguin – and how to order them, contact us at the appropriate address below. Please note that for copyright reasons the selection of books varies from country to country.

www.puffin.co.uk

In the United Kingdom: Please write to Dept EP, Penguin Books Ltd, Bath Road, Harmondsworth, West Drayton, Middlesex UB7 0DA

In the United States: Please write to Penguin Putnam Inc., P.O. Box 12289, Dept B, Newark, New Jersey 07101–5289 or call 1–800–788–6262

In Canada: Please write to Penguin Books Canada Ltd, 10 Alcorn Avenue, Suite 300, Toronto, Ontario M4V 3B2

In Australia: Please write to Penguin Books Australia Ltd, P.O. Box 257, Ringwood, Victoria 3134

In New Zealand: Please write to Penguin Books (NZ) Ltd, Private Bag 102902, North Shore Mail Centre, Auckland 10

In India: Please write to Penguin Books India Pvt Ltd, 11 Panscheel Shopping Centre, Panscheel Park, New Delhi 110 017

In the Netherlands: Please write to Penguin Books Netherlands bv, Postbus 3507, NL–1001 AH Amsterdam

In Germany: Please write to Penguin Books Deutschland GmbH, Metzlerstrasse 26, 60594 Frankfurt am Main

In Spain: Please write to Penguin Books S. A., Bravo Murillo 19, 1° B, 28015 Madrid

In Italy: Please write to Penguin Italia s.r.l., Via Felice Casati 20, I–20124 Milano

In France: Please write to Penguin France S. A., 17 rue Lejeune, F–31000 Toulouse

In Japan: Please write to Penguin Books Japan, Ishikiribashi Building, 2–5–4, Suido, Bunkyo-ku, Tokyo 112

In South Africa: Please write to Longman Penguin Southern Africa (Pty) Ltd, Private Bag X08, Bertsham 2013